The Corset
and other forms of control

Short stories by
Mary Bridson

 FriesenPress

Suite 300 - 990 Fort St
Victoria, BC, V8V 3K2
Canada

www.friesenpress.com

Copyright © 2019 by Mary Bridson
First Edition — 2019

All rights reserved.

No part of this publication may be reproduced in any form, or by any means, electronic or mechanical, including photocopying, recording, or any information browsing, storage, or retrieval system, without permission in writing from the publisher.

This book is a work of fiction. Names, characters, places, and incidents are either products of the author's imagination, or are used fictitiously. Any resemblance to actual events, locales, or persons, living or dead, is entirely coincidental.

"Of Cabbages and Kings" was originally published in the Newfoundland Quarterly, Vol.92, No.2, Fall 1998.

"Collision Course" was originally published in The Cuffer Anthology, Vol.II: A selection of short fiction. ed. Pam Frampton. St. John's: Killick Press, 2010.

Cover artwork by Heather Bale.

ISBN
978-1-5255-4435-4 (Hardcover)
978-1-5255-4436-1 (Paperback)
978-1-5255-4437-8 (eBook)

1. Fiction, Short Stories (Single Author)

Distributed to the trade by The Ingram Book Company

Acknowledgements

I am grateful to my late parents, Jean and Alec Dickie, who gave me my first typewriter and started me on this path to publication when I was ten.

The annual Newfoundland and Labrador Arts and Letters Competition was a major incentive in the writing of many of these stories, as was the Telegram Cuffer Prize Competition. I am sure many aspiring authors are equally grateful for the opportunities they offer.

I also thank my husband for his indulgence of my many hours spent scribbling, for the occasional idea that I stole for a story, and his loving support over the years.

Table of Contents

THE CORSET — 1
A young Victorian wife and mother, constrained by the conventions as well as the physical fashions of aristocratic society, finds freedom and self-respect in this amusing tale of intersecting lives.

OF CABBAGES AND KINGS — 23
This is a comic tale of a would-be prizewinning gardener in Newfoundland and his animal protagonists. The antics of Rex, Leo, and Caesar are interspersed with skipping rhymes, which summarize the action.

THE ANGELS' SHARE — 37
A woman returns with her son to the Scottish island where she grew up. What she discovers, when revisiting memories of her two best friends and the events that changed her life, surprises and disturbs her.

BOLLOCKS COVE — 59
Abandoned by her English mother when she was four, a young girl in a Newfoundland outport feels like an outcast. She tries to make contact with her by sending messages in bottles out to sea.

BIDING HER TIME — 69

A young elephant witnesses her mother's killing by ivory poachers, which condemns her to a life of loneliness and pain. She finally finds love and respect, but her new life is shattered when she recognizes an enemy from her past.

MAIDEN GRIMM — 87

A young girl's life seems to parody several different fairy tales, as she moves naively through puberty.

COLLISION COURSE — 101

The lives of an eccentric old lady, her grandson, a developmentally delayed man, and a professor and his dog, collide in a Newfoundland outport.

TABULA RASA — 107

A mother is devastated by the sudden death of her dependent adult son. Her daughter, with whom she shares a difficult relationship, tries to make amends.

MIRACLE BOY — 117

A young boy survives, physically unscathed, a senseless massacre at a school in outport Newfoundland. He becomes the focus of media attention and a charitable fund, but his life, and the lives of the other survivors, turn into further tragedy over time.

SCALPING THE LORD   139

The increasingly bizarre development of the Catholic Church's great money-maker and ticket to Heaven, the plenary indulgence, is fancifully described.

THE GREY HAVENS   153

An elderly man living in St. John's is haunted by memories of sickness and death and the miseries entailed, and he decides to take control of his own passing with minimum impact on his family, and on his granddaughter in particular.

AUTHOR/*SUBJECT*   171

The author and subject in this story are engaged in a surreal struggle for dominance, told from both points of view.

FLIP   187

This quirky tale is told back-to-front and inside out at the whim of the author, and features two gamers who meet by chance in fog-bound Cape Spear.

The Corset

"No, Molly, stop! Don't, it's hurting, I can't breathe."

"Now, M'Lady, you know it's for your own good. One more pull. Hold steady now." Molly braced her knee against her mistress's back and pulled the lacing of the corset even tighter. "There! That'll do, M'Lady. You look quite trim now. You have to get that loose flesh back under control. Hold everything in its right place. I could tell you tales that'd make you weep, of some of the women I've seen. Six months after the birthing, and their wombs hanging out between their legs. God's truth, I swear! And paps swinging over their navels like a cow's udder. Perish the thought you'd ever look like that, M'Lady."

Caroline shuddered at the graphic description. Molly used coarse language on purpose to shock her, she knew, and it worked every time. To hide her embarrassment, she wriggled and tugged at the thin cotton chemise trapped under the whale bone, casting a furtive glance at the long glass. The corset was pale blue figured silk, embroidered with pink roses and little tufts of darker blue forget-me-nots. Plaited pink and blue satin ribbons decorated the shaped top, which gripped her breasts too tightly, and a froth of white lace blurred the stiff edging. Her stomach was cramped and flattened by the sturdy metal busk encased in deceptively soft silk, which was complemented by long rows of whale bone at either side and all round the back. It was a French creation, a new gift from her husband.

* * *

Molly had insisted on a corset from the moment Caroline was allowed to get up from her bed, a few days after the baby was born. She laced her in every morning, a little tighter each day, bruises and tearful pleas notwithstanding. It was a race against time to get her mistress in good shape by the opening of the season in late September.

Confined to bed, Caroline had been at the mercy of Molly and the nurse, who decided when she was fit to see and hold her own child. Now at least, she could slip into the nursery regularly to sit and watch the wet-nurse suckle her son, change his soiled cloths, bathe, and cradle him. That first afternoon she had plucked up the courage to tell the nurse to go and have tea with the other maids, and that she would look after the child for an hour. The baby was sleeping, and the nurse grudgingly agreed, provided she was alerted as soon as he awoke.

Alone at last with her little boy, Caroline had felt a great surge of love and responsibility for this tiny soul, flesh of her flesh. She stroked his warm cheek, which caused him to turn towards her, sucking gently in his sleep. She smiled. His little fist uncurled and stretched, and she held out her finger, which he grasped tightly. She rocked his hand to and fro and tried to remember the lullaby her own nanny had sung to her. He startled and frowned, pouting his lips, and then began to whimper. She quickly pulled away her hand, worried that his cries would bring the nurse and a scolding, but the sudden movement woke him up. He started to cry in earnest, and she began to get flustered.

She was suddenly aware of the prickling in her breasts and then the wetness bringing relief from their swollen hardness. Mothering instincts overcame all her upbringing, and she struggled to free her breast from the confinement of the corset. She pulled off her smock and fumbled with the laces at the back, but in her haste she tugged them into a knot, and the harder she strained, the tighter it grew. The baby was getting impatient, and she tried to pull the corset round so that she could get at the laces, but it trapped and squeezed her breast, making her yelp with the sudden pain. She yanked the breast free and picked up the baby, holding him awkwardly against her, but he was in a rage now, thrashing his head from side to side, and couldn't find her nipple. She couldn't believe how loudly such a small, red-faced, squirming bundle could yell. Tears of panic and frustration sprang to her eyes.

Moments later the baby was whisked out of her arms and onto the shoulder of the nurse, where his sobs snuffled out. Within minutes he was sleeping peacefully again.

"He's settled now, M'Lady. His next feeding isn't due for another two hours, so I suggest we leave him alone."

The scorn and anger in the nurse's eyes were withering. Caroline's tiny spark of pride in mothering her baby was extinguished, and she was again a naughty child caught playing with the ornamental porcelain dolls in her grandmother's collection. She knew her presence in the nursery from now on would be closely monitored, and there would be no more private moments of intimacy with her child. Molly was called to rearrange her clothing and adjust the corset, and then she was led back to her own room in humiliating silence.

* * *

Now that this evening's lacing was over, Caroline stood meekly enough, stepping into her drawers when told, and lifting her arms to have the bustle buckled on, and the various petticoats and brocaded satin evening gown lowered over her head. It was a matter of pride with Molly that this dress from the bridal trousseau should still fit her mistress. Caroline perched on the velvet-covered stool, the bustle hanging over the edge, while Molly vigorously brushed out her hair and pulled and twisted it into the mandatory bun and ringlets. Finally her face was washed, creamed, and powdered, and a touch of rouge applied to her cheeks and lips.

"You look like the ghost of Lady Jane, M'Lady. Let's put a bit of flush in your face. It's all that bleedin' after the birth. Takes the colour right out of you."

In dressing rooms all over the city, ladies were going through similar rituals, emerging stiffly from the manipulations of their maids to step into carriages and be trotted away to dinner parties, balls, and card games in each other's houses. Lady Caroline Bowles was to be one of the hostesses tonight, her first appearance on the social scene since her condition had become too indelicate for decency. At least one of her guests was very interested in her performance. The Countess of Chatsbury, Caroline's aunt by marriage, had been sorely disappointed by her own daughter-in-law, who had produced nothing but a couple of bloody miscarriages since her marriage the year before. Young girls these days, so out of shape.

Molly was acutely aware that her mistress would be under careful scrutiny for signs of weakness, pallor, and loss of figure, which was why she played the tyrant. She had her reputation as a lady's maid to maintain in the downstairs gossip halls of the establishment.

* * *

Reputation was a different matter for Sadie Perkins. She didn't give a beggar's knuckle for her good name in the servants' quarters, but she was proud of her notoriety among the gentlemen's clubs in the City. Madame Sophie's Boudoir was whispered and winked about over the port, and she picked up many new customers from the emerging ranks of fresh-faced public school graduates, as well as their fathers and uncles.

Lord Randolph Bowles, heir to the overly long-lived Lord Nile of Porthampton, and successful dabbler in banking, had been paying regular visits to the Boudoir off Cheapside for the past several months while his wife was off limits, and indeed on several occasions before that. Earlier that afternoon he had walked boldly up to the narrow terraced house in the little mews, no longer casting furtive looks over his shoulder as in the early visits, and tapped briskly on the door with his cane. A young maid opened the door, took his coat, gloves, and cane, and showed him into the parlour. She smiled sweetly and said that she would inquire whether her mistress was at home. If he had strained his ears hard enough as he waited, which of course a gentleman doesn't do, he would have heard a murmur of voices, a passage of feet past the door, and the click of a lock opening and closing.

"Old Randy's here, Sadie. D'you want to see him today?" The maid was on very familiar terms with her mistress.

"What I *want*, Anna, is a nice cuppa tea and a couple of muffins, but I suppose that can wait. Let's see . . . Randy's a dresser rather than a stripper like his nibs" – Sadie jerked her thumb in the direction of the lately departed client – "so I'm all ready for him. Just give me a mo' to freshen up. Oh, and tell Mary to put the kettle on, we won't be more than half an hour."

Anna poured some warm water into the bidet, checked the various garments lying about the room, and laid them neatly on the bed. Then she went to fetch Lord Randolph.

"Ah, Randy, mon chèri. Come in, entrez. You are just in time to help me wit' my dressing, non? I cannot lie around like zis all day!" And with no hint of a blush for her atrocious fake accent, Madame Sophie stretched her creamy white arm along the back of the love-seat and uncurled her legs, lifting one high over the other to reveal a brief glimpse of erotic shadow beneath the folds of her thin gauze chemise.

Lord Randolph bent to kiss her outstretched palm. "But of course, Madame, that is why I am here. Would you step this way?"

The ritual began. The maid handed the items one by one to Lord Randolph, who then dressed Madame, with many a caress and squeeze of her intimate parts along the way. First came the corset, his favourite piece. Crimson satin pleats concealed the delicate bone stiffeners, which curled into the waist then flared over the hips. Each lace-topped silk cup was boldly embroidered with a black rose in full bloom, revealing a large red garnet at the centre, and embraced by long-necked swans with seed pearl eyes. The black velvet-covered spoon busk curved deeply down over the belly, and from each side dangled black lace-trimmed suspenders, a novel invention, to which the white silk stockings would be attached. The adjustment and lacing of this fine contraption to Madame's satisfaction took some time, and Lord Randolph was in a high state of anticipation by the time he was fumbling with the last button on her long, crushed velvet skirt. He remained bowed to the floor while Madame and her maid took turns to chastise him for his incompetence.

"Zat will do for today, bad boy. You must practice some more. Per'aps next week? Anna will arrange it, n'est-ce pas?" Lord Randolph was ushered out.

Sadie gave a big sigh, expertly whipped off her working clothes with minimal help from Mary, and, wrapped in a warm flannel dressing gown, she relaxed with her cup of tea. Another day, another few guineas earned. She thought she would take the evening off. It was the start of the social season after all, and most of her clients had other duties to attend to.

* * *

Caroline was uncomfortably aware of all the eyes appraising her entrance to the drawing room, but to most of those watching she appeared aloof, straight-backed, and almost ethereal in her slender figure and virginal colouring. The gentlemen were pleased to have one of their fairest ornaments back on view; the ladies were mixed in their admiration, envy, and disbelief. Lord Randolph was exceptionally delighted with her and looked forward to later that evening. The maid, Molly, had informed him with great satisfaction that his wife was once more available for nocturnal visits.

Caroline accepted a small glass of sherry. The Countess of Chatsbury insisted it would bring the roses back into her cheeks and help her constitution.

"You look so frail, my dear. I'm afraid you will hardly be able to manage a baby." The irony of this remark was not lost on those standing near, who turned aside to smirk. The Countess' own management style and failure to produce a grandson was well known. But the truth of it was a painful stab in Caroline's already crushed ribs.

If standing had been uncomfortable for her, sitting at table for a five course dinner was excruciating. She could barely lean over enough to scoop up her game soup, and she toyed with the baked whiting, lamb cutlets, partridge pie, and roast fowl as they succeeded each other in slow procession. She chewed the odd mouthful but was hard pressed to swallow without frequent sips of wine.

The conversation of the two gentlemen who pinned her in on either side was not designed to hasten the evening. The Earl of Chatsbury was interested only in giving her graphic descriptions of the breeding problems of his elite fox hounds, problems remarkably similar to those of his daughter-in-law. The young man on her other side was seeking to impress her, and thus indirectly her husband, with his knowledge of the minutiae of banking and insurance. During a brief lapse in these expositions, she caught the eye of another young lady across the table and received an encouraging smile and sympathetic raising of an eyebrow. Her husband's second cousin, Louise, had just arrived in town from her country estate, having had a baby herself a few months before. Caroline wondered if she was also laced so tightly, but she didn't seem inhibited in the way she relished every dish.

Lord Randolph could barely conceal the hungry and proprietary gleam in his eye as he surveyed his wife at the far end of the table. She looked as delicate as a harebell caught amongst thorns, and he adored her, as he had from the moment he first saw her.

"Yes, she's a fine looking girl, Randolph, but brittle as glass. You shouldn't breed her again for a while. It could break her." The Countess on his right did not miss a move. She was always frank in her opinions, but her nephew was startled by the observation. He thought his wife looked perfect. She had a healthy blush on her cheek by now, and she seemed to have come through the throes of childbearing in excellent shape. Sour grapes, dear aunt? he silently mused. Caroline's waist was as trim as ever, was it not? Much better than his dumpy cousin Louise, who seemed to have let herself go.

When at last the dessert was laid out, little dishes of fresh and preserved fruits, ratafias and ginger biscuits, sweetmeats, and dainty lemon ices with mint, Caroline felt some relief. She was a little dizzy from the wine, and closed her eyes briefly, nearly missing her cue to rise and lead the ladies to the drawing room, while the gentlemen passed the port. She leaned against the fireplace lintel, unable to sit again quite so soon, and forced a smile. Louise came over to join her and whispered in her ear.

"My dear, you look as though you need to loosen your laces, and soon. What was your maid thinking of, pulling you in so tight! You hardly ate a scrap of dinner, and that's no good for a nursing child."

"Oh, but I'm not nursing the baby, Louise! Heavens, I'm not some common milkmaid, you know. Molly, my maid, tells some quite awful stories of women whose figures were totally ruined – "

"Well, it's not hurting mine, is it?" Louise smiled.

"Oh, I'm sorry! No, of course not! I didn't realize you were . . . In fact, I was rather envying your appetite at dinner and thinking how well you looked, considering."

"Considering I'm not trussed up like a turkey, you mean? I gave up those wretched iron-plated waspies as soon as I started getting heartburn in my third month. The relief was enormous. And I still only wear a padded bodice with a few bones to relieve my back. You should try it."

Caroline blushed. "Oh, but I have to keep my waist. I mean my husband – Sir Randolph – this is how he likes me. He . . . he wouldn't even look at me when my belly was all swollen. I'm afraid I shall just have to learn to put up with it. It will get easier, do you think?"

"My poor Caroline, it's obvious that man adores you! Do you really think it is the corset that has him all sheep-eyed every time he looks at you? Think better of yourself. He'll love you with or without a waist the size of a swan's neck.

"Come, you must visit me tomorrow, and bring the baby. I'll show you what I mean about not needing those stays. Do you know, there was a woman in America who actually wore some sort of trouser out on the street? Imagine being able to ride a horse properly, like a man! We really are such fools to confine ourselves this way. We must take charge of our bodies, Caroline!"

The Countess was not particularly pleased to see the cousins gossiping happily together in the corner. As the premier guest, she felt she merited more attention from her hostess. Rudely inserting herself between them, and with a curt nod to Louise, she took Caroline's arm and led her away across the room.

"Ah, my dear, allow me to rescue you from that bore. I hope she wasn't preaching to you about the new fashions she has espoused. She has a real bee in her bonnet about it, so I've heard. And you can see for yourself how unflattering they are."

"Oh no, Countess, not at all! In fact she is going to show me some of her magazine articles tomorrow. It sounds quite fascinating. And I would say she looks very fit and healthy, even without a proper waist." Caroline bit her lip at this inadvertent slip of etiquette, but the Countess smirked.

"Well, dear, you don't need to worry about *your* waist, do you? You'll disappear entirely if you pull yourself in another notch. But that's what it takes, I suppose, to keep your husband's interests at home."

"I beg your pardon, Countess?"

"I mean, my dear, that you will distract him from his visits to Madame Sophie's in Cheapside."

The roomful of women went very quiet. More than one of them had heard of Madame Sophie, but it was backstairs gossip, not fit for the drawing room. Caroline, however, seemed not to notice the subtle change in atmosphere.

"And who might Madame Sophie be, please?"

Even the Countess hesitated in the face of such apparent naiveté. She drew back from administering the knock-out punch.

"Oh, she's a . . . a lady of charity, my dear. She takes poor girls in off the street, feeds and clothes them, and finds them work. I believe Lord Randolph and some other gentlemen support her work – anonymously, of course."

The awe-struck silence following this remarkably ambiguous explanation was quickly disrupted by the entrance of the gentlemen, florid and animated by the quality of Lord Randolph's port, and ready for further entertainment. Card tables were set up, a few gathered round the pianoforte, and the evening resumed its normal pace.

As soon as etiquette permitted, Caroline made her excuses to her guests and her husband and retired to her chambers, pleading a slight indisposition. The guests did not linger long. They could see that Lord Randolph was somewhat anxious about his wife, and they made their farewells with sympathetic nods and murmurings: it was very soon for her ladyship to be up in the evenings; it must be very tiring; looking wonderful, but mustn't overdo it.

Molly was full of gossip from the kitchen quarters as she helped Caroline remove her finery, piece by piece. It seemed that she had triumphed, and the other ladies' maids had been suitably impressed by her ladyship's slender carriage.

"Molly, for pity's sake, get these wretched laces undone before I faint away. You may be happy, but I've spent a most miserable evening."

Molly's chatter, however, continued apace, and she found a dozen other things to attend to before the corset. Then there was a sudden rap on the door and Lord Randolph walked in, to Molly's evident relief.

"That will do, Molly. I will attend to your mistress now." In fact, Lord Randolph had previously arranged with the maid that he would see to his wife's disrobing that night, and that on no account was she to remove the corset before he arrived.

"That was close," thought Molly, with a private grimace. "But good luck to him, the mood she's in tonight."

Lord Randolph surveyed his wife, standing before him in the exquisite French corset he had chosen for her. She was shy and confused, her features flushed, and her hair brushed out in long, lazy curls.

"Enchanting! Perfect! So . . . so virginal."

Caroline's emotions were running high. She was embarrassed to be suddenly standing nearly naked in front of her husband, who normally did not enter her chamber until she was tastefully attired for bed. The wine and words from the evening were still buzzing in her head, and the corset bones were digging into her sides.

"Please, sir, I beg you, help me get this thing off." Caroline reached for a shawl to cover herself, and turned her back to her husband.

"No, no, my sweet! No hurry, and don't hide yourself. Let me . . . let me touch . . . " Lord Randolph reached for her hand and pulled up her arm, while he ran his fingers gently down the patterned silk, traced the line across her swelling breasts, and curved his hand down past her waist to the ribboned edge of the garment. "How soft you are," he murmured, "but firm, and so elegant. Magnificent!"

Caroline, for one awful moment, thought that he was addressing the corset.

"No, please, undo the laces for me and let me out."

Reluctantly he began to pick at the knots. He eased the bodice and the crushed chemise away from her body, then drew a sharp breath. Caroline looked down – and was horrified! Where the corset had held her in its clutches, her skin was indented, a row of angry red bites all round her waist, and a bruised welt across the top of her breasts. She burst into tears.

"Molly! Fetch Molly! Oh, please don't look, go away! I'm so ugly, go away!"

But Lord Randolph could not take his eyes off the marks. He was fascinated by the pattern, like a garland of engraved rose petals, and he felt his excitement growing. He pulled Caroline towards him, but she collapsed in his arms in a dead faint. He swore under his breath in a most ungentlemanly manner, picked up his limp wife, and laid her on the bed. He took one long, last look . . . then pulled the bell swag for Molly and left the room.

"Oops! Maybe we did overdo it a bit, M'Lady." Molly looked rather sheepish as she applied a warm bread-and-water poultice to the bruises and wrapped a moist flannel cloth around the waist. She tucked her mistress into bed with warm soothing words, that all would be well in the morning.

"Please . . . tell my husband that I do not wish to see him again tonight." The tears welled up once more. It had been a very disturbing evening.

* * *

All was not well in the morning. Caroline went straight down to the nursery in her dressing gown and demanded to hold her baby. The startled nurse maid handed her the child, but remained hovering at her elbow until told to go and sit down. Caroline was inwardly amazed that she could command such authority, and was beginning to enjoy it, until her son started to fuss and cry. She had to admit defeat again, or at least inexperience, and let the nurse take him back. But before she returned to her room, she gave orders that he was to be made ready for an outing, as he would accompany her on a visit to her cousin after luncheon.

Molly was more subdued than usual. She had got a wigging from His Lordship last night, and this morning Her Ladyship had a definite gleam in her eye, so Molly did not object when Caroline slipped her hands up under the plain white stays to prevent her from lacing them too tightly.

* * *

The afternoon visit to Cousin Louise proved most interesting and informative. Caroline discovered a whole new world beyond her experience, acquired a few necessary tips, and absorbed several strategies to help her realize her newly-awakened ambitions.

A few days later, a new seamstress arrived at the house, and appointments were made to see a couple of new couturiers. Molly's nose was decidedly out of joint. Her protestations that no good would come of these floppy new fashions were ignored. But the final straw came a couple of weeks after that, when she was summoned to go through Her Ladyship's wardrobe with her.

"Molly, I want all these dresses with tailored waists put on one side, and we'll do away with the bustles too. The chemises and blouses are probably fine, and Katerina can alter most of the petticoats. And I'll just keep a couple of pairs of the lightest stays; the new padded bodices are so much better. Get one of the other maids to help you pack up the rest, and then we have another visit to make."

"*All* the other corsets, M'Lady? Even the – "

"Yes, Molly, *all* of them. Oh, and if there are any other old aprons or bibs or smocks that the household can spare, put them in too."

* * *

The next afternoon, Lady Caroline Bowles' carriage rolled down Cheapside and turned into the little mews whose name she had discovered by careful enquiries through her cousin's equerry, a servant too discrete to ponder the reasons for such a strange request. Caroline set Molly down to go and arrange the desired interview.

Anna opened the door. She took one look and let out a great squawk.

"Molly Roberts! Is that you, girl? Come back to lord it over us poor things, 'ave you?"

"Shut up," hissed Molly. "And you can wipe that silly grin off your mug, Anna Campbell. Don't ask me how or why, but Her Ladyship wants to see

Madame Sophie about a donation. For her *charity* work, d'you see? Now get in there and tell Sadie to put her act together."

The two ladies were ushered into the parlour to wait, while across the hall Sadie and her girls tidied up as best they could, bursting with giggles and speculations. Madame Sophie hastily donned a demure costume – she chose the French schoolmistress number – and prepared to greet her visitor. She decided against the false French accent.

"Lady Bowles, such an honour. And Molly, my dear, how are you making out? I hope you find her satisfactory, M'Lady. Your husband was most kind to give her such an opportunity, serving a *real* lady."

Molly, already flustered, turned red as a beet.

"Molly? I had no idea you were one of Madame's charity girls." Caroline looked genuinely startled. "How . . . kind and thoughtful of my husband. I look forward to hearing all about it later. But now, Madame. I was told about your work by my aunt. She said you helped poor girls off the street, and that several gentlemen, including my husband, privately supported you – your charity, that is. I would very much like to donate some cast-off clothing to your cause if you will accept it. Anonymously, of course."

Sadie looked her straight in the eye, but Caroline did not flinch. Sadie smiled.

"Thank you, M'Lady. You're too kind. I'll see what I can do with it. Anonymously, of course."

Back in her carriage, Caroline fiddled with her bonnet strings to hide the trembling of her hands and her shortness of breath, but gradually she regained control of herself. She need not have worried. Molly was huddled in her own corner, eyes cast down, wondering how in heaven's name she was going to answer questions from either Her or Him about today's can of worms. She was in a right old bind, and for the moment she could not see any way out of it.

* * *

Sadie and her girls were already picking through the boxes with a practised eye. Some items they threw out for the rag bag, others they put on one side for suitable alterations. Then Anna made a great discovery.

"Hey, Sadie! Look at this, then!" And she held the blue embroidered corset up against herself and twirled around.

"Blimey, that's a bit of quality stuff," said Sadie thoughtfully. "Looks brand new, too. Now why would Lady C. be throwing that away, I wonder? . . . I wonder." A wicked gleam came into her eye as she arched her brows in mock innocence. "What do you t'ink, mes amies? Shall we give our chèr Randy a little t'rill tomorrow? Let 'im buckle

Madame Sophie up in zis charming little 'arness for a change?"

The girls tittered. Sadie Perkins, as always, was on top of the situation.

The End

Of Cabbages and Kings

> Scratch, scratch, scrabble, scratch,
> Leo's in the cabbage patch.
> Quick! Quick! Grab a stick,
> Give that pesky cat a flick!
> Whack – yowl! Scratch – howl!
> Another undecided match.

Leo streaked down the path and up into a neighbour's tree, leaving Rex clutching his bleeding arm and formulating a hundred and one feline finales under his breath. He surveyed his mangy vegetable garden. The cabbages were barely the size of a fist and laced with caterpillar tracks. The soil was dusty from the hot spell of weather they had enjoyed in late August, and it smelt strongly of cat.

Leo stretched his tawny limbs along the tree branch and inspected his sabre claws. He gave his immaculate fur a couple of rasping licks to smooth the ruffles, then turned his amber eyes full beam on Rex. The hint of a Cheshire smile twitched his whiskers.

With a sigh, Rex walked over to remove an old sneaker that was lodged in the twin trunks of a chokecherry tree. He had never yet made a direct hit with this weapon, but he was accurate enough to disturb Leo from his early morning ablutions among the raspberry canes. Rex did not consider himself a gardening enthusiast. He didn't tune in regularly to Canadian Gardener or belong to the local association of amateurs, but he did think it worthwhile to grow a bit of fresh, flavourful food and brighten his yard with daffodils and pansies. Since Leo had appeared in the neighbourhood, however, this happy dabbling was fast becoming a major commitment to strategic warfare. This season's campaign he had already conceded to Leo. Everything he harvested looked a little stunted, and the soft fruits needed rinsing, sniffing, then rinsing again. Even the turnips were suspect, dug from a minefield of cat turds, and the odd one exhibiting furrowed scars down its side.

"Next year," Rex vowed to his wife, "I will not stand for this. That damned cat is a public nuisance, and I will take all measures necessary to eliminate it."

"You are not putting out poison or traps, Rex. I will not have the SPCA knocking at our door or the neighbours giving us the cold shoulder. If you want to keep that animal at bay, you will have to outmanoeuvre it. You surely won't admit that a mere cat can beat you at a game of wits!"

So the battle lines were drawn and the rules agreed. Leo spent the winter months curled up behind the warm stove of a tolerant foster home, with periodic excursions into the woods to hunt sleepy birds and mice. Rex laboured in his garage with wire netting, do-it-yourself books, seed catalogues, and potting soil.

* * *

Next spring, as soon as the frost had loosened its grip, Rex began to scrape the old soil off his vegetable garden and trundle it off to a far corner, where he had decided to start a compost heap. He had built a solid base of patio slabs on a gravel bed and then cemented six or seven layers of bricks around it, with gaps to allow the heap to breathe. He carefully layered the old soil, fresh grass cuttings, weeds, and household waste, dosed it with fertilizer, and hosed it with water. He inspected it daily and was quite surprised at how fast the volume of waste compacted after a few hot days. He had high hopes for this gardening season. Leo also gave it careful inspection, under cover of darkness, and decided it was worth an occasional visit, particularly after he had detected the hidden kitchen scraps. In fact his scrabbling in the heap probably helped the rotting process by circulating air, but what did he care. Rex cared, when he found bits of egg shell and cheese rinds scattered about the garden, but he had more important problems to ponder.

The main priority was the vegetable patch itself and the construction of a cat-poof barrier. Rex had studied several handyman manuals from the library and had come up with a solution to suit his pocketbook. Now he discovered the drawbacks. In most civilized North American backyards, there is enough soil to sink a fence post a couple of feet deep and secure it with a spot of concrete. In Newfoundland, the soil has an average depth of an inch and a half above bedrock, or it consists of several feet of black bog muck liberally seasoned with boulders just below the thrusting pickaxe. He had to compromise. A curious structure appeared, of wire netting threaded with spindly spruce trunks and roped to trees at not quite right angles. In a couple of places it was actually supported by metal fence posts leaning a little drunkenly out of stone pits, with a latched gate slung between them.

However, before he completed the final side of this fence there had to be something worth protecting. At ridiculous expense, considering the foregoing measures, he ordered in truckloads of A-1 sifted top soil, well-rotted horse manure, and peat, and spent a sweaty weekend mixing it together with bags of lime dust. The resulting bed was at least six inches higher than its predecessor and looked fit for a princess, peas and all. He could practically hear the buttercups straining their runners to get into it and the dandelions puffing themselves up for a soft landing. He raked it with loving care and gave it a final pat before heading inside for a bath.

"And next weekend, I'll finish the fence and get the cabbages pricked out," he promised himself.

Leo was impatient to investigate this new improved litter box. It was delightful how easily his claws could plough through the loam, and he had half a dozen pits dug in no time. He lay back to catch the early morning sun, luxuriating in the soft, warm, smelly soil. It was perhaps a little too comfortable, and Leo dozed off for forty purrs.

"Gotcha, you son of a . . . son of an alley cat!" Leo's dignity was shattered by the impact of a size twelve walking boot, and he fled the battle ground with a screech before Rex could cut off his retreat. An hour later the bed was remade, and the final stretch of wire netting in place. It looked a bit shaky, but that would probably be a better deterrent to a cat burglar.

* * *

A couple of weeks passed in relative peace. Rex sowed peas and beans, along with carrots, lettuce, beets, and turnips, and pricked out two long rows of cabbages from seedlings lovingly fostered on the kitchen window sill. Leo decided that the compost heap was much more accessible, and he left the vegetable patch alone.

"Well, I have overcome the cat problem," Rex boasted to his wife. "The garden's coming along really well. I think I might enter the vegetable show this year. Those cabbages have such a good start I could even win first prize."

"And pigs might fly," muttered his wife under her breath, but she was glad to have him happy again.

* * *

All might have been well if Rex and his wife had not driven down to the beach one evening in early July for a breath of fresh air. It was capelin spawning season, and the shallow water along the gravelled shore was thick with silver fish. The sea seemed to be boiling at the edges as the capelin writhed and wrestled for their moment of ecstasy before dropping exhausted on to the beach to die.

Children were scrambling among them, shrieking and grabbing them by the tails to plop into a beef bucket, and watching them swim desperately round their shrunken ocean. The fathers were gathering fish in bigger buckets and nets dipped into the shallows, anticipating a tasty fryup and dried, smoked snacks. At the end of the beach, an old man was shovelling the dying fish into a barrel in the back of a horse-drawn cart.

"That's a fine haul you have there."

"Yes, b'y, I like to get a couple of loads into the garden this time of year." He winked at Rex. "Nothing like it for the cabbage and turnip, you know. I grow the best darn crop in the Cove." Food for thought!

The next morning, Rex was down on the beach raking dead capelin into garbage bags and loading them into the trunk of his car. His wife would not readily forgive him for thus contaminating her weekly groceries for the next month, but at that moment it was visions of prize cabbages as big as pumpkins that floated before his eyes. Back home he carefully dug a trench between the rows of young cabbages, another by the turnips, and buried the pungent cargo. Unaccountably, he completely overlooked the natural affinity between cats and fish.

His error was readily apparent the next morning. What a feast for a cat whose appetite had been piqued by compost hors d'oeuvres! Turnips sprawled out of their moorings as if hit by a squall. Fish bones, tails, and glassy eyes were scattered among the limp-leaved cabbages. And in the middle lay a very fat cat, flicking the last shiny scale off his whiskers before tackling the problem of squeezing back under the fence, which he had climbed so lithely an hour or so before.

He didn't have long to contemplate the problem. Rex was out of the house in pajamas and bare feet, arms flailing like a windmill, and hell-bent on murder. Leo was not prepared to sacrifice a life at this time, and with a supreme effort, he pressed his swollen stomach to the ground and clawed his way under the wire netting. Rex grabbed for his tail and felt it slither through his fingers. Leo fled into the bushes and was gone before Rex could get out of the gate and round the fence.

> Mister King
> Went fish-ing
> Caught a load of cap-e-lin.
> In the trench
> What a stench!
> Leo dug it up ag'in.
> Vex'd
> Rex
> Fat
> Cat
> SCAT!

Rex was not fit to be spoken to for the rest of the day. He toiled in silence to remove every trace of dead fish from the garden and drop it back into garbage bags. He heeled the turnips back into their beds and shored up the cabbages, then he gave the whole garden a good soaking. By evening most of the plants had perked up again, and Rex was out with the repellent spray, which promised to deter cats or dogs from trespassing where they were not wanted. Leo decided it was in his best interests to lie low for a while.

The cabbages recovered from their ordeal, and a week or two of cool, wet weather really brought them along. Then the sun came out again, and with it another problem. Butterflies. They might look innocent enough fluttering about the cabbages with their dainty, virginal wings, but they were almost more deadly than Leo. Under the leaves of almost every plant they left their hidden time-bombs, all set to go off while Rex was away.

* * *

Returning from a week's camping trip, Rex's first concern was to check for Leo damage; no paw prints, no earthworks, no smell. But his self-satisfied smirk faded as he caught sight of the air-conditioned leaves on the closest cabbage plants, and he was soon immersed in a massacre, squishing little green caterpillars between his fingers till they dripped. The damage assessment from this first bombing raid was not as bad as he feared. The hearts of most cabbages were still intact and potential prize winners. But he would have to get his air defence systems in place before the next attack.

Rex spent that evening constructing painted cardboard cut-outs of flying objects, supposedly birds, but more like air-ships with fins. He wrapped each one in clear plastic tape to make it waterproof, then he anchored it to a piece of fine string with a blob of the sealing wax that had gathered dust in his desk drawer for years. Next day, he strung several lengths of garden twine across the vegetable patch from fence to fence and tied the cut-outs at intervals along them. They bobbed and twirled from their red wax eyes quite unrealistically in the breeze – any cabbage white butterfly with a modicum of intelligence would avoid them like the plague.

However, a cat with an irresistible urge to pounce on a moving object was a different matter. Leo watched in fascination from the neighbour's tree, never a whisker twitching, and finally began to move with the stealth and purpose of a Serengeti lion along the furthest limb. He paused to calculate the distance – then sprang into the air with a suppressed hiss of triumph. He landed amongst the cabbages with a string of hapless, flapless birds in a tangle at his feet. He scratched out their bloodshot eyes but soon lost interest in the game. He relieved himself of his tension and then, clawing his way out under the fence by the same route as he took after his fish dinner, he stalked down the path with his tail held high, acknowledging with a jaunty flick the awe in which the real birds held him as they hopped up out of his way.

* * *

At the end of August, Rex stood with mixed feelings before his rows of cabbages. The flower show was the next day, and he had to choose his prize specimen. It was not exactly an easy task. He walked along between the rows, dismissing one cabbage after another. These ones had been partially uprooted in the fish episode and were somewhat stunted. Those had been badly squashed in the subsequent kerfuffle and were lopsided. The odd one had succumbed to the ministrations of a well-disguised caterpillar. That one had split its sides at the antics of Leo with the scarifiers, and another had lolled its head to one side in stupefaction. Of all the plants there was just one, it seemed, that had survived unscathed and was now the undisputed monarch of the patch. Rex heaved a sigh of relief and returned to the house to fetch the large kitchen knife with which to perform the sacrificial rite.

Leo was not present for this crowning ceremony. He had grown bored with the summer campaign and had wandered off to greener pastures. There was a house up the road which had been for sale most of the summer, when its occupants had followed their livelihoods to the mainland. The grass had flourished in that time, unmanicured but dandified, and Leo found it perfect cover for creeping up on starlings, juncos, robins, voles, or whatever other unsuspecting creatures were roaming about in it.

This afternoon he had come across a most interesting object; quite large and hairy, and heaving slowly up and down. He stalked up behind it, making barely a rustle in the long grass, and, without waiting to consider the consequences, pounced with all claws unsheathed. The large hairy object sprang to life with an alarming deep-throated growl. It shook Leo off its back like a dead leaf and turned to glare with squidgy eyes and a wrinkled nose at the trespasser. This was the new proprietor of the overgrown garden, protecting his humans' investment, and Leo decided not to dispute the matter at this time. He rolled over onto his toes and took off round the corner, but the bulldog was not finished with him yet. Leo ran down the road with the dog wheezing along behind him, and in his desperation, he fled into Rex's garden for cover.

"Caesar! Caesar, come back here!" The new neighbours did not want to start out with a reputation for uncontrolled animals, but Caesar had a point to make. He was not going to let anyone think they could treat him like a fool on his own property and not pay for it.

Leo climbed the wire netting like a circus pro and dropped down among the cabbages. He bolted under the spreading leaves of the largest plant and curled up into an orange smudge. Caesar floundered after him into the garden, through the flower beds and raspberry canes, and came up against the fence with a whack that flattened his face more than ever. Undeterred, he hurled himself again at the barrier, and this time one of the fence posts popped out of its rocky moorings, and the netting collapsed beneath his weight. Caesar sniffed his way around the cabbages to pick up the scent, and suddenly the patch exploded in a snarling, hissing ball of fur, teeth, and claws.

Rex ran outside, knife in hand, and was rooted to the spot in horror. Leo suddenly broke loose and flew up and over the far side of the wire netting to safety in the neighbour's tree. Caesar, his pride satisfied, picked his way back over the broken fence and padded down the driveway with barely a glance at Rex.

Leo stretched his tawny limbs along the tree branch and inspected his slightly bloody claws. He gave them a couple of rasping licks, then turned his amber eyes full beam on Rex. The hint of a Cheshire smile twitched his whiskers. And down the road, the neighbourhood skipping bee was already working on its latest rhyme . . .

> Caes-ar! Caes-ar!
> Snuffle-nosed wheezer.
> Catch that cat? You're too fat,
> Bet the fence will squeeze yer!
> Caes-ar! Caes-ar!
> Leo's such a teaser.
> Don't be dense, squash the fence
> And get that amber greaser!
> Caes-ar! Caes-ar!
> Rex is in a seizure.
> His cabbage bed's all in shreds
> Coleslaw for the freezer!

The End

The Angels' Share

As the spirit lies undisturbed, it gradually absorbs subtlety and character from the cask and the surrounding atmosphere. But it also loses some of its sharpness and fire as a portion of it evaporates – the angels' share.

- - - - - - - - - - - - - -

The Paps of Jura hid themselves demurely behind swirls of mist as the ferry nosed its way towards the islands. Jennie stood in the bows, watching the contours of her childhood take on a clearer definition. She found her fingers tracing the slight hollows of the scars on her cheek and brow and quickly thrust her hand back in her pocket.

"Mom! The cafeteria's closing, and I'm starving. Aren't you frozen out there?" Rory called impatiently from the shelter of the cabin. She knew he would rather have stayed and explored Glasgow after her mother's funeral. Or even better, be back with his friends in Toronto, where it was still sunny and hot. But her husband David had arranged this "return to her roots" as a special treat. Perhaps he thought it would settle her down, lay the ghost, as it were. Her mother had never set foot on the island again in all those years, and nor had she, respecting her mother's feelings. But now she couldn't contain her curiosity.

Rory joined her on deck when the ferry began to swing surely and gently towards the ramp. He scrutinized the precision and efficiency of the crew as they docked and unloaded without a bump. Probably the highlight of the trip for him, thought Jennie. A city boy, born and bred, with a passion for science and machinery. Whereas the very smell of the salty shoreline and the rain sweeping the peat bogs set her nerves tingling.

They took the bus across the island. The bell heather was in full bloom, later than the mainland, and brightened the muted browns and greens of the moors. A small field of ripening barley was suddenly lit by a stab of sunshine on their left, an oddity in this landscape of sheep, cattle, and peat.

"Look," she said. "They're still trying to grow their own. It's only for show, so the distilleries can say they do the whole traditional process on site. But even in my day the grain was imported." Rory didn't even glance up from his computer game.

* * *

She remembered other fields of barley. She and Meggie used to tunnel into the centre out of sight.

They squeezed the sweet pulp from the green barley grains with their teeth, risking cut lips from the sharp husk, while telling each other secrets. Who had kissed who in the schoolyard, whose mother owed money at the shop, whose father was away in jail on the mainland and not fishing like they said. And how they thought babies were made. They had explored their own bodies, trying to make sense of the snippets of information they had picked up. That was before Duncan had come, of course.

* * *

Now they were crossing the vast peat bogs that stretched across the middle of the island. In the distance, the mechanical cutters were at work, and stacks of peat stood along the roadside waiting to be collected for the Maltings. Rory took a bit more interest.

"We used to cut it by hand," said Jennie. "It was hard work, gave you blisters. Nice smell in the stove though, not as sooty as coal. Real low tech compared to our nuclear power plants in Ontario!"

"They produce a lot of hydroelectricity in Scotland," Rory said, surprising her. "But I suppose it's a bit flat around here. They could probably use wind power though." Together they stared out over the landscape, each lost in their own thoughts.

* * *

It was her dad's favourite punishment for the Midges. That was his nickname for her and Meggie, because they were a constant nuisance, pestering the men with questions and getting into places they shouldn't be. He would send them off with a couple of peat spades and orders to fill a basket each. As they got older it was two or three baskets each. However, it didn't do any good. Meggie was always coming up with new ideas for mischief, and after Duncan's mother started work at the distillery, there were three of them to pool resources. Duncan was even more spirited than Meggie.

* * *

They got off the bus in the town and searched for the B&B up and down the row of whitewashed houses, with their prim square windows and tight-lipped doors crowding the pavement.

"There it is, Mom, on the corner," said Rory. "Tigh-na-eilean. Dad said it means House of the Island." The name was neatly printed on a board above the door. A well-dressed, good-looking girl in her twenties, with deep blue eyes and black curly hair, appeared as they knocked, and welcomed them in.

"Hello, I'm Morag. You must be Mrs. Steinberg. I'm the only one here at the moment, but I'll show you your rooms. Then I'm afraid I must go. I'm working at the distillery this summer and I have to give the next tour."

"Can we tour the distillery, Mom?" said Rory. He had not taken his eyes off the girl since they arrived, Jennie wryly noted.

"You're very welcome, but I'm afraid children are not allowed to sample the end product." The girl smiled. Rory flushed, but held his own.

"I'm thirteen, not a child! And I don't care about that, I'm interested in the process. My grandfather managed a distillery – "

"Not this one though," Jennie hastily interrupted. She wasn't sure she was ready for this yet, but Rory was looking for her support. "I suppose we can do the tour. I haven't anything else in mind for today."

A small group of middle-aged American and Japanese tourists, and a couple of young bikers from Glasgow, huddled around Morag as she led them through the distillery yard and into all the various buildings, explaining the process of malt whisky production. Rory was fascinated. They edged round the wire mesh floor in the kiln under the pagodas, where the germinating barley was dried by the peat fires below. They peered into the huge mash tuns where the grist, or ground malt barley, was mixed with hot water to produce the sugary liquid wort.

"We Scots are very resourceful. The solid dregs from the mash tuns are sold back to the farmers – as cattle feed." Morag's solemn face was belied by the twinkle in her eye. "We have the happiest cows around."

They paraded past the wash stills where the fermentation was frothing up the sides.

"Whew! What a stink!" Rory seemed to voice a common opinion. And then his face lit up as they entered the lofty hall, where the giant copper stills rested their fat bellies and bent their necks to the condensers. This was where the real skill lay, testing the quality of the spirit as it was run through the padlocked spirit safe, taking only the middle portion, and running the rest back to be distilled again.

"Only the excise man has a key to the lock, for obvious security reasons," Morag told them. Jennie wondered if that had always been the case. The group moved on out towards the sheds by the shoreline, where the oak sherry casks held the liquor for however many years it took to mellow and mature.

Jennie was no longer with them. She had caught sight across the yard of a tall, broad-chested man with a head of curly ginger hair. She pulled up sharply, her heart leaping. He looked just like the photo of his father, the absent soldier, which he had always carried in his pocket.

"Duncan? Duncan MacLean?" Why such a shock? Had she not expected them to be still on the island, as she probably would have been were it not for the accident? It was a small place, she was bound to run into them soon enough.

The man turned, and a pair of faded blue eyes stared from under devil's eyebrows. Now she wasn't so sure. There was something strange about him.

"I'm sorry . . . I thought you were someone I knew."

"Aye, I know yon voice. It used to belong tae Jennie Campbell."

Jennie blushed and instinctively covered her scarred cheek. Then she noticed the white cane tucked under his arm. She didn't know what to say, so she blustered on.

"Yes, I'm back on a visit. First time, actually, since . . ." Silence. "My mother just died in Glasgow, and my husband thought I might like to – "

"Ye're married then."

"Yes. Rory – my son – is with me . . . And you?"

"Oh, there you are, Mrs. Steinberg, we thought we'd lost you. Hello Duncan." Morag came hurrying over. "Children have to be accompanied at all times, you know, safety regulations. Isn't that so, Duncan?"

"Aye."

"Mr. MacLean here is our chief nose – in charge of quality control. If you'd like to come this way, then?"

"Maybe we could meet later, a drink?" Jennie couldn't just let it go at this, after so long.

"I dinna drink." Duncan turned abruptly and walked through the archway towards the still house. She noticed he didn't use the cane. He must know this place like the back of his hand.

Morag eyed her appraisingly. "Mr. MacLean is a reformed alcoholic. He has the best nose in the business, but he never lets a drop pass his lips."

* * *

Rory didn't appear to notice his mother's distraction as they ate their dinner in the local hotel. He was explaining to her the intricacies of whisky making and how the differences in shape and angle of the still pots affected the strength and flavour, ignoring the fact that she had lived and breathed distilleries as a child.

* * *

She didn't know what exactly had happened. She was under sedation for several weeks and had extensive surgery. When she was finally able to grasp her surroundings in the Inverness hospital, she learned from her mother that her father had been killed in the fire, and that they were beginning a new life away from the island. She had been hurt that no letter or enquiry had come from her friends, and then the hurt had turned to anger, so that she didn't write to them either. As her new life developed, and her mother made it clear that the subject was taboo, she gradually let go of the past.

She remembered her first meeting with Duncan. His mother was the new secretary, and he was with her when Jennie came by her dad's office after school. Her dad told her to go off and show Duncan round the place. There were no regulations then about unaccompanied children. Duncan was shy that first day but seemed to take in every word she said. He certainly learned everything about the ins and outs of the distillery in no time. When she showed her prize to Meggie – for having your very own boy to trail around behind you was definitely worth some points – there was a row. Meggie called her a traitor for showing Duncan some of their shared secrets, and she hit back by saying Duncan was more fun. That had led to a series of dares and adventures, which they all found exhilarating, as Meggie and Duncan vied to outdo each other. And that was also when they really learned the facts of life, Jennie recalled. A dare that nearly froze their butts off in a little bothy out by the peat bog one November afternoon.

* * *

"Mom! The lady said did we want our bill." Jennie came back to the present with a start. They went back to the B&B and let themselves in. Rory wanted to watch TV in the little guest sitting room, but Jennie said goodnight and went off to her own room. Memories of childish escapades were far more entertaining than anything the box had to offer.

* * *

Next morning at breakfast, Morag appeared with steaming plates of porridge and a special smile for Rory. She whispered something in his ear, but he didn't blush, which Jennie thought curious. She was about to ask what was going on when the elderly landlady herself appeared, another character from her past.

"Mrs. Macdonald, what a pleasant surprise! I hadn't realized this was your place that my husband had booked. It's a lovely house you have now, very comfortable, and a wonderful view." Jennie was blustering on again, while her mind was grappling with this new turn of events. What was Meggie's mother doing living here in town? The farm behind the distillery in the old village had been in their family for generations. So where was Meggie? And who exactly was Morag? She had assumed she was the daughter of the house.

"I'm sorry, do I know you?"

Jennie was taken aback. Duncan had recognised her right away, in spite of his blindness. Or maybe because of it.

"It's Jennie – Jennie Campbell. It's been too long, I know, but my mother – "

"Jennie!" A succession of emotions passed over Mrs. Macdonald's face. Then she smiled politely and said "Well now. And you are living in Canada. I hope your mother is well? We lost touch, as you must know." How much charge there was in those few words! Jennie found herself defending her mother and explaining the circumstances of her visit. No explanations were offered in return. She took the plunge.

"And Meggie? I'd love to see her and chat about old times."

"Margaret keeps to herself these days."

"Oh . . . Is she here in town?"

"No, she lives at the farm still. With her father." Obviously this was dangerous ground.

"Perhaps I can call in on her, then. I was going to look at the old place before we leave."

Mrs. Macdonald smoothed down her apron and looked away.

"Perhaps better not to. Margaret took it very badly, you know. Everything that happened. She doesn't like to talk."

There was an uncomfortable silence. Morag glanced from one to the other, eyebrows raised, then smiled at Jennie, breaking the tension.

"I was telling Rory that I have some more diagrams and pictures of the distillery he can have for his science project. I could take him over there this morning if you would like to have some time to explore on your own?"

She was a shrewd observer, that one, Jennie thought. She wondered how much Morag understood about what was being said, or rather, unsaid.

* * *

No one else got off the bus at the old stop. The tourists, on their way to the first distillery visit of the day, looked with idle curiosity at the ruined sheds and dilapidated pagoda, threatening to topple into the sea. The cobbled yard was softened by moss, and delicate blue hare bells grew from the cracks in the long burnt timbers of the malting floor. Jennie watched the bus disappear down the narrow winding road then turned back through the years. She walked around the old place, her feet guided by her memories. She found a bannister rail and a few steps climbing into thin air, all that remained of her father's office. The lofty walls of the still hall now sheltered nothing but sagging pipes and torn wires. The copper pots and condensers had been salvaged after the fire, no doubt. Even the jetty, where the matured casks were once loaded, was rotting under the weight of the swaying bladder wrack. The damp-floored warehouse, its roof blown off, no longer held its mysterious liquid treasure.

* * *

The spirit safe in the still hall had been their first objective that evening, more than twenty five years ago. Meggie had thought it only fair that they should sample the local product that fuelled the island economy. Her Presbyterian parents didn't even allow a nip at Hogmanay, and they were all naturally curious. Jennie thought her father would probably have a key in his office, and Duncan volunteered to hunt for it. She and Meggie waited outside in the road, keeping watch. He wasn't gone long.

"Forget it," he grunted. "Your dad's in the office." He took off, shoulders hunched against the rising wind, but Meggie was not so ready to quit.

"Then let's have a go at the really good stuff, out in the warehouse. You're not chicken are you, Duncan?"

Duncan could never ignore her taunting, and a short time later they were back with a paraffin lamp, matches, a chisel, hammer, and hand drill. The night watchman was dozing by the stove in his hut at the front of the warehouse. They climbed up the back wall from barrels stacked along the jetty and in through a vent by the roof, a route that they had discovered months ago. It was pitch dark inside. Jennie went first, as she was the smallest, and Duncan then handed her the tools and the lamp, which she lit on the third attempt. She balanced astride the rafters holding the lamp, while Duncan squeezed through the gap and swung himself down. She dropped the tools to him but stayed perched where she was, watching. She could tell he was not in a good mood, and it made her wary.

"Tell me when it's ready for swigging," Meggie whispered. "I'll keep a look out just in case."

Duncan gave up on the hand drill very quickly and instead began chipping at the wooden bung of one of the casks. His temper was rising, and soon he was smashing the cask with the hammer. It spurted all over the floor. He cursed and started swinging at the next cask, smashing that too. Jennie caught her breath in alarm.

"Hush, you idiots!" hissed Meggie. "Hey, what's happening there?"

Jennie flung her leg over the rafter and twisted round, holding on briefly before dropping to the floor. She jarred her ankle and fell headlong into a cask, jolting it off its chocks and sending it rolling towards its neighbours. The lamp had fallen with her, and the last thing she remembered was a sheet of flame as the flood of spirit ignited.

* * *

"So it is you back again," said a familiar voice behind her. Jennie whipped around. A stout, middle-aged woman in black skirt and stockings, with a plaid shawl around her shoulders, stared down at her.

"You recognised me then," said Jennie. "Duncan is the only other one who has." Her hand strayed once more to her cheek.

"Morag told me you would be here. That's a nasty scar."

"I was just revisiting the scene of the crime," Jennie blurted out to hide her embarrassment. She was looking in vain for the skinny, spirited, daredevil confidante of her youth. Could this really be Meggie?

"They should demolish all these ruins," Meggie said, turning away. "It isn't safe. They're an eyesore."

"I think you're right. I wasn't really expecting to find them like this. A bit of a shock. I knew there was a fire of course, and that my father pulled me out, but I didn't realize how great the damage was."

Meggie gave her an odd look.

"You never replied to our letters after. We never knew for sure whether you were OK."

"But I never got any letters. I thought you didn't care. My mother said . . . My God, do you suppose she hid them from me? But why would she do that? I don't understand."

"Come and have a cup of tea. I think we both need to sit down and talk."

They made their way across the road and down the track to the Macdonald farm.

"Morag seems a very nice girl. Very bright too." Jennie wasn't sure how to ask the question that really gnawed at her.

"Yes. She's doing her Masters in chemical engineering at Glasgow University. She just works at the distillery for pocket money when she's home."

"Is she your . . . sister?"

"No, she's not my sister. Heavens, Jennie, my Mum is a bit old for that! I was her bonus child, remember? My brothers were nearly grown when she had me. Mum took Morag in out of charity. My Dad wouldn't have anything to do with it, seeing she was conceived in sin. Told her he wouldn't have the child in his house." Meggie glanced sidelong at her. "Does she not remind you of anyone – Morag?"

Now Jennie was really embarrassed. The likeness and familiarity between Morag and Duncan had not escaped her. She tried a different tack.

"You decided to stay here with your father, then, when your mother moved into town? Was that after Morag was born?"

"He's a hard man, my Dad, but he needs a woman around. My Mum can cope just fine. Always good in a crisis. Morag's mother knew what she was doing when she left her in Mum's wash basket."

Meggie was in the kitchen now, putting the kettle on. Jennie felt she would burst if she didn't ask.

"Did you and Duncan not get married then?"

Silence. Then a muffled explosion of noises that Jennie could not interpret. Laughter? Sobs? Anger? Frustration?

"You think Morag is a love child of me and Duncan?" The scorn in her voice was withering. "My dear girl, not a chance in hell. He was *your* slave, Jennie, surely you knew that? He only ever had eyes for you. He's been waiting all these years for you to come back. And to thank him."

"Thank him? For what?"

"For pulling you out from under a pile of burning barrels! No, your mother lied to you about that too. Your dad didn't even know we were in the building. I'm not sure you even realize that there was more than one fire that night. It got pretty windy, and the peat furnace under the malting floor flared up out of control. Old Boozy Bob was the only man on duty, remember? And he was snoring in his hut and never noticed a thing till I gave the alarm. They said your dad had sent the rest of the men home early from their shift. Deliberately."

This was more than Jennie could handle right now. She glanced at the clock and made fumbled excuses. She had to catch the bus back to town and collect Rory for the trip they had planned to the museum across the island. In her haste to get away from the dark picture that was emerging, she did not arrange any further meeting.

* * *

Jennie was faintly amused to find everyday tools of her childhood in the museum display, and there were names she recognized among the donors, but Rory was bored by everything except the old mill machinery. They toured the north end of the island, visited Celtic crosses and old grave yards, the nature preserve, and gift shops. A continuous blanket of drizzle did nothing to rouse their enthusiasm, and both were silent and distracted. After tea, Rory mentioned, a little too casually, that Morag had offered to show him her blueprints. Jennie tried not to smile, and he hastily explained that it was her Master's degree project for an improved whisky blending system, and he scuttled off to her room. Jennie, left to her own devices, decided she had better finish what she had begun with Meggie that morning.

* * *

As she walked down the track to the farmhouse, Jennie smelled burning and saw a haze of dark smoke hanging in the damp evening air. Her heart skipped a beat, and she hurried round to the backyard. Meggie was there, feeding a pile of old school exercise books into the last flickers of the burning rubbish heap. She watched Jennie approach, as she ripped another book in half and threw it on.

"I had to hear the rest," Jennie said simply. "What is it you're burning?"

"I figured these were a waste of time now," Meggie replied. "I started them a few months after the fire, when we didn't hear from you. Duncan took to drinking, and I wrote my heart out. Love poems. To a lost love."

"Oh, Meggie, I'm so sorry. I wish Duncan could have got over me, and it had worked out between you."

Meggie bristled with sudden anger.

"It wasn't Duncan, you idiot! These poems were for you. You were my lost love, Jennie Campbell. What a bloody fool I've been, mourning you all these years, when you were out there making a cozy new life for yourself." Meggie turned away, and strode towards the house.

This time, Jennie resisted her natural instinct to flee these painful revelations. She picked up the only book that had escaped the bonfire and flipped through the pages. She read a short poem, and then another, and before long she was engrossed. This was not the teenage angst and melodrama that she had expected. She was deeply moved by the flow of words and subtlety of feeling. The book was dated many years after the fire. Meggie must have kept up her writing over all that time, and she had developed into a truly fine poet. Jennie wondered if she had ever published anything. She had been full of ambition as a kid, burning to see the world and make her mark. Jennie quietly pocketed the book and followed Meggie into the kitchen. If she was ever to find out what had really happened, it was now.

"You're right, Meggie, I am a complete idiot. I really had no idea, we were so young. I should have written to you. But I believed what my mother told me, and it upset her when I asked questions. Please forgive me. But I must know all the truth now. Why did my mother lie, and what was my father up to that night?"

Meggie sat at the table, head in her hands. She didn't look up.

"You know when Duncan went to look for the key to the spirit safe? It wasn't just your father he saw in the office. His mother was there too, and they were both naked. It was her that your father saved, before the fire trapped him.

"When Duncan's dad returned from his tour of duty and found his wife pregnant, he took off, abandoned her and Duncan both. His mother couldn't take living in the village any longer, what with the icy stares and holy cursing and everything, so she did a disappearing act too, leaving Morag with my Mum.

"Yes, in case you hadn't worked it out – Morag is *your* sister, yours and Duncan's."

* * *

Jennie let herself back into the B&B very quietly, but Morag was waiting for her.

"I don't mean to be rude, Mrs. Steinberg, but I think you should catch the early ferry tomorrow. You seem to have upset all my family by your visit.

Better not to disturb the past, I think. You can't recapture what's lost."

She handed Jennie something wrapped in a brown paper bag.

"Duncan dropped this off for you. He said he'd been saving it for a special occasion, but there won't be one. It's a bottle of the '79. It's worth a fortune, one of the best malts ever laid down. It's from one of the last barrels saved from the fire at the old distillery."

* * *

The sun glimmered through the watery haze between the ferry and the mainland as they headed east. Rory was in the cabin, pouring over the technical sheets and specs that Morag had given him, planning a project for the next science fair that would blow away the competition. He wondered if the barley grains and piece of peat he had smuggled in his luggage would pass inspection, and whether his mother would let him use that bottle in his display. Maybe a miniature filled with apple juice would be safer.

Jennie gripped the rail tightly, staring resolutely ahead. She hoped the bus was waiting, and they could make it back to Glasgow in time to change their flight. As the sun rose above the mist and the sky cleared, she turned back briefly. The Paps had finally shed their tattered shawls, and

their gently rounded summits stood bold and bare above the islands. That's how she would remember them.

The End

Bollocks Cove

The first time Clavering tried to send a message across the ocean in a bottle, the suspense lasted only a day. Next morning when she came down to the beach, she found her bottle lying on the high water mark, tangled in kelp. At first she thought it was a miracle that a message had been sent back to her so soon, but then she was only six years old. She didn't know anything about the swirling currents in the cove that could smash a small boat against the rocks and leave it as flotsam on the tide, or the undertow that could swallow up a person forever.

* * *

Clavering's mother had met her father in St. John's, at a bar off Duckworth Street. He was a fisherman from the southern shore, in town to buy some tackle. She was an international student at the university, having a bit of an adventure before settling down to teach primary school somewhere back home in England. They hit it off famously, a study in contrasts, blurred by alcohol. In no time, he had wooed her and carried her off to Bollocks

Cove, to be a mother to his son and a lover for the cold winter nights when he missed his Colleen. She had no-one close enough to care back in England, so maybe she thought she would find a new family in the new found land.

Bollocks Cove! Elizabeth hadn't believed his explanation of how the outport got its name, but when she saw the tapering rock stacks – bottle rocks – that guarded the entrance to the narrow neck of the cove, she laughed and conceded its merits.

Their daughter was born less than a year later. By then Elizabeth had decided that Newfoundland outports were rather like English villages: picturesque and friendly on the surface, but they closed ranks to prevent any penetration by outsiders. She was miserable, penniless, and home-sick, and almost as an act of defiance, named her baby after her own native English village. Rocking her daughter, cooing her name, she felt some small warm link to her old life beyond the impassable horizon.

* * *

"My Nan says I can stay with her anytime I want." Connor pulled a face and stuck out his tongue.

"My Nan says – "

"You don't have a Nan, Clay. You don't have anyone now your Mom's gone."

It was true. Elizabeth had disappeared from Clavering's life when she was just four, and no-one talked about it, not even her Dad. Her stepbrother, Connor, had all his mother's relatives at hand to look after him, but they only grudgingly helped her father out with his alien daughter. Dear Mother of God, she wasn't even Catholic! By the time she was six, she had learned to pretty much fend for herself when her Dad was out on the boat.

Then one day after school, Connor had told her about messages in bottles. He had heard from a friend that a kid down the shore had thrown a bottle into the sea a year ago, with his name and address, and had just had a letter from a family in Ireland that found it on the beach. All the way over the ocean on the other side! Next time she wandered down along the landwash, she looked at the sea with new eyes. Maybe it wasn't just a barrier. Maybe it could be her friend. The message she sent was very simple: "Cum hom mommy luv Clay." She didn't tell anyone what she had done, and when the bottle didn't go anywhere, she wondered whether Connor was lying to her again. He was always getting her into trouble that way. She bit her lip, wouldn't cry, and went back home.

* * *

In May all the children made Mother's Day cards to take home.

"Who you givin' yours to, Clay?"

"Where's your Mom, then?"

"I ain't never seen her – is she in the graveyard like Connor's Mom?"

Clavering fought back. "I do so have a Mom! I'm sending it to her. I know where she lives. She just don't want to come home yet, that's all."

That afternoon, while her Dad was out and Connor was at his Nan's, she rummaged in the shed looking for her father's empties. She rolled her card as tightly as she could and stuffed it down the neck of a large glass rum bottle with a screw top. This time she climbed up the steep cliff path at the end of the beach and ventured right out to the point, where she wasn't supposed to go. Hanging on to an old wizened stump of black spruce, she flung the bottle out to sea as hard as she could. She didn't really care where it went, as long as it didn't come back. She had no idea who or where her Mom was, but she wanted to get rid of that useless card.

* * *

Clavering spent a lot of time wandering along the landwash. Most of the other kids hung out near the fishing rooms and the wharf, kicking a ball around, catching sculpins with homemade rods and borrowed line, generally larking about. Sometimes they would come down to the beach, turning over rocks looking for crabs, popping the seaweed bladders, or skimming pebbles on calm days. They occasionally teased her, but mostly they just ignored her.

She was crouched down by the sea edge watching a jelly fish floating transparently in a tidal pool, when she heard the voice behind her.

"Your mother liked to walk down here all the time."

She spun round and saw a man sitting propped up against the side of the nearest rock stack, beached by the receding tide. He had a six-pack beside him and seemed settled in for the afternoon.

"She used to collect the urchin shells. Said she liked to decorate her plant pots with them. Them and the little quartz pebbles."

Clavering stared at him.

"You don't live here," she said. "Who are you?"

"Well now, I guess I'm your uncle, of sorts. Connor's uncle, Riley. You don't remember me?"

"Connor said you went away to work, in Canada."

"That's right. Fool's game, this fishing, now the stock's gone. I earn big money out west."

"What you doing here then?"

"Just home for a visit, nosey-poke. Haven't been back for a couple of years or more."

"My Mom's gone."

There was a long silence, and Clavering went back to poking in the pool. When she looked round again, the man had his head down, hands over his eyes.

"Are you crying?"

He raised his head and looked away from her.

"We all needs to cry sometime, lass. But some of us never learn how."

"Tell me more about my Mom."

Clavering learned more things about her mother that afternoon than she had ever heard from her father or brother, or anyone else for that matter. Her mother used to sing to her, old English ballads, and carry her around in a sling. Her favourite colour was pink, and she used to make clothes for Clavering's teddy out of scraps left from her sewing. She went berrying on the downs behind the cove, and Riley helped her pick. He worked night shifts at the fish plant, so he spent lots of afternoons with them. Elizabeth had disgraced herself with his family, though. Riley's mom had prepared a dish of cod tongues for her when she first arrived, as a sort of welcome, and Elizabeth had choked on them and thrown up all over the table.

"She said she was allergic to fish, but no-one believed that was possible. And when she tried to make a Jigg's Dinner for us all – a kind of penance, she told me afterwards – no-one could eat it, 'cause she'd trimmed all the fat off of the meat and it was as tough as old boots! She was cack-handed in the kitchen, that was what she called it. True enough!"

Her mother loved the beach, just like Clavering did; picking over the driftwood, trying to identify shells and beach plants, listening to the beat of the waves and the sighing of the pebbles. But she was scared of the sea, couldn't swim, wouldn't go out in the boat. Her Dad got quite cross with her about that, he could have used some help with hauling the pots at times. Colleen had used to help him, Riley told her, before she got sick. Elizabeth had a garden, but she didn't plant cabbage or carrots or anything useful like that. She tried to grow hollyhocks, or some such, and other flowers she knew in England where she came from. They didn't do too well in Bollocks Cove though.

Clavering didn't know whether it made her angry or sad, now that she had more than a photograph on which to build a portrait of her mother. What she didn't understand was why her mother had abandoned her.

"Do you know where she went?"

The man had stopped talking and was gazing out through the bottleneck of the cove. He didn't reply at first, but pulled himself up, tossed the last beer bottle into the waves, and shrugged.

"I can't find the answer to that one either," he said softly. And then he walked off, up the steep cliff path, and out of her sight.

Five brown beer bottles lay in a row on the lip of the beach. Clavering picked one up and walked home with it hidden under her fleece. She didn't tell Connor she had seen his uncle.

* * *

Next morning she came down to the beach again, clutching the bottle. Inside it had a message to her Mom, painstakingly printed, and it was sealed with a plug of dough and some duct tape. She passed the rock pool, dried up now, with a piece of shiny skin like plastic film stuck to the bottom – all that remained of the jelly fish. A scattering of brown glass shards lay at the foot of the rock stack. She climbed up the cliff path and, holding on to the stumpy black spruce, again flung her bottle far out into the green marbled water. The pebbles groaned and rattled on the beach below. The wind was picking up, and black clouds were rolling in from the south. There was no sign of Uncle Riley.

* * *

The big storm blew in overnight, even penetrating the Bollocks, washing flotsam up onto the wharf, and plastering the windows of some fishing rooms with kelp. A couple of boats that hadn't been pulled out of the water were smashed, and towers of crab pots toppled and scattered in the road. A few shingles had blown off, and some basements were flooded where the stream backed up behind loosened boulders, but on the whole the Cove had a lucky escape.

Clavering shivered in her bed all night, thinking about her mother – her shells, her love of flowers and the beach, and her fear of the sea. Drifting into a dream world, Clavering was clinging to the spruce stump, reaching out to clutch her mother's hair as she swam out to sea past the rocks. Her mother turned and smiled at her, waved goodbye, and blew her kisses as she vanished into fog. Clavering woke with a great sob, and she lay in the dark listening to the storm as her breathing quietened.

"I promise!" she whispered. "I'll keep sending the bottles to you. So you know I'm still here. And you'll come back." She rubbed her knuckles fiercely into her eyes to quell the tears.

* * *

A great black-backed gull glided along the disheveled beach in the early dawn, scavenging for urchins and other delicacies churned up by the storm. It scooped up a prickly ball and soared high over the cliff path to drop it on a rock and smash the shell. Its eager eye was momentarily distracted by a glint of light in the narrow ravine on the other side of the point. It followed the emerging rays of the sun fingering along the waves towards a shallow cleft near the bottom of the sheer rock face. There was a cache of broken glass, scraps of paper, a red tinsel heart, a dirty pink rag, some bleached bones. Nothing of interest to the gull, which flew back up to its perch on the old spruce stump to eat the freshly cracked urchin.

The End

Biding Her Time

The world was a huge, warm, moving bulk of wrinkled flesh. For the first three years of her life, the elephant was never more than ten metres from the gentle nuzzle of a trunk, the comfort of a teat, and the shelter of solid legs. She followed her mother across the thorny scrub lands, grassy plains, and in and out of mud holes and drinking pools. When she was a little older, she ventured further afield, but never out of sight of her mother. The others – aunts, cousins, sisters, brother – followed her mother too. The world was good, and it surrounded the elephant with warmth and security. And then the world was torn apart.

One evening, her mother stepped into a hidden trap, a pit dug in the middle of a centuries' old elephant path through the thorn trees. She roared and stomped, pulling rocks and tree branches down on herself as she struggled. Two shots rang out. A high-pitched scream of rage and pain echoed through the still, warm air and slowly faded. The rest of the herd panicked and fled. The young elephant stood alone by the pit, looking down on the collapsed and crumpled body of her mother.

Before she could begin to make sense of what had happened, she felt a thick rope round her neck and hobble chains clamped on to her legs. Out of the trees emerged a tall white man in khaki, limping slightly, with a gun under his arm. His piercing green eyes rested briefly on the young elephant, and then he gestured to the group of black natives that had bound her, as he snapped out his orders. They ran to fetch axes and a saw, then scrambled down into the pit, where they hacked at her mother's face and sawed off the beautiful ivory tusks that she had wielded so proudly. They cut off the feet, and even the tail, and packed the bloody trophies into baskets lined with leaves, which they slung into the back of a landrover. The young elephant herself was then bundled into a covered truck, and the vehicles drove off into the deepening gloom.

Half a life time seemed to pass confined in that truck, as she rolled against the sides, banging her head on the struts as it bumped along the rough track. Once she heard gunfire in the distance, but the truck gathered speed, and all her concentration was focussed on keeping herself upright.

Dawn was just breaking in a flush of flamingo clouds along the horizon when the truck pulled up at last. The elephant was pulled down the ramp, her legs shaking, her stomach churning, her whole being a constant throbbing ache. She was hustled into a small pen at the back of the compound, where there was a water trough and a pile of hay. No-one came near her for a long time, save to top up the water and throw in more hay or old wrinkled vegetables and peelings. She was hungry. She had not been fully weaned and found the hay difficult to digest. She was also terribly, fearfully, lonely. But there was nothing she could do, so the elephant bided her time.

* * *

One morning a young boy appeared on top of the mud wall of the pen, swinging his legs against the side as he watched her. She approached carefully, wondering at this first two-legged being to show any interest in her. He didn't move away but continued to stare at her. She recognised something in his dark eyes: a reflection of her own fear and loneliness. Then he smiled. She hobbled forward a few more steps and raised her trunk, tentatively exploring his face. He gasped, reached out and grabbed her trunk, yanking it away from his face, while kicking her in the throat with his boot. The sudden pain made her squeal, and the boy continued to kick at her while twisting her trunk. Two men came hurrying out, and the boy quickly let go.

"Are you OK, Todd? Did she hurt you? I'll give her such a beating – "

"No, Dad, it's fine. She was going to bite me, but I can handle her." The boy grabbed his father's whip and slashed at the elephant's head with it. She backed away and stumbled to her knees, to the boy's obvious delight.

" Oh look, Dad! I made her kneel down! I could train her to do tricks. Can I have her, Dad? Please? The other boys would be pretty impressed. No-one else has an elephant."

Todd was a difficult boy for his father to deal with. The ivory dealer had married a demure young Chinese girl on one of his trading visits to Shanghai, and Todd was the only issue of their short-lived union. He was a loner, small and rather delicate, very obviously different from the other boys in the colonial school, and his father suspected he was bullied and ostracised; but then his own colleagues also looked askance at the boy. There were very few Chinese in East Africa at that time. If an elephant would bring him out of himself and give him something to boast about, then an elephant he should have. After an hour or so of haggling with the green-eyed man, the dealer and his son left the compound with a carefully concealed shipment of merchandise, and the elephant in a trailer.

* * *

The elephant's new home was a paddock previously occupied by race horses. Todd showed a great deal of interest in her at first. He would appear in the morning, smiling and cooing at her, holding out a banana in his hand. She hobbled up to him – the hobble chains were not removed, for safety's sake, and had started to chafe one of her ankles. She reached for the banana, and then he whipped out a club from behind his back and beat her with it, screaming and shouting until she turned her head away and retreated. Another time, he would come up and begin to prod her with a long stick towards a mounting block in the paddock. She stumbled forward, and he smiled and laughed and threw her an apple. As she leaned over to retrieve it, he yelled at her again. This sort of behaviour continued every day, and the elephant was now paralysed with fear and indecision whenever he came into the paddock. Nothing she did seemed to please him, and she hardly dared come up to him, however much he cajoled her with treats and soft words. But that made him angry too. Training an elephant was harder than he had realized.

Two other boys came with him one day. They were laughing and fooling around, but Todd was looking very serious and determined.

"Show us then, Slanty Eyes" said one of the boys. "Let's see these famous tricks of yours."

"Yeah, Elephant Boy," sneered the other. "Make him sit up and beg."

Todd stared hard at the elephant, shouted a command, and slowly held out a banana, her favourite treat. She hesitated, but recognizing the look of desperation in his eyes, she overcame her fear and approached the group. However, he didn't let her take the banana but instead flourished the whip and cracked it about her ears.

"That's not much of a trick," said the taller boy. "Anyway, she's hobbled. Bet you don't dare get close to her in case she kicks your butt!" They laughed again.

Todd flushed. He threw down his whip, jumped over the fence into the paddock, and strode towards the elephant, his temper flaring. The elephant shuffled quickly backwards, hit her sore leg against the mounting block, and stumbled forward again, away from the pain. Todd twisted sideways to avoid her. He slipped on fresh dung and was suddenly under her feet. She had him completely at her mercy, and the temptation was overwhelming to release her own frustration, confusion, and anger. But she saw that his fury had now turned to an impotent dread that kept him pinned to the ground, and the memory of her own moment of helpless terror by the hidden pit flooded back. She turned away, contempt and pity, but no longer fear, in her eyes, and slowly she shambled over to the far side of the paddock. There the elephant stood, swinging her trunk back and forth, biding her time.

* * *

The boy did not come near the paddock again, and after some time the elephant was once more loaded into a truck. Another long, bumpy journey, but on better roads, taking her farther and farther from the plains of her infancy. They passed through heavy forests, alongside wide, sluggish rivers, in and out of towns and villages, and eventually pulled into another large compound. There was a lot of activity here, sounds of other animals and men at work. Maybe she would find her old herd members.

"What you got there, Bill?"

"Elephant. Young orphan. Fellow said he got her from a farming friend, who found her roaming his property. Had it for a pet, but doesn't want it now. We picked it up for a song. Should be useful if we can get her trained up."

They unloaded the elephant into a small enclosure. After a while, a man in a white coat came in and started to poke and prod her, peer into her eyes and ears, and run his hands all over her body. He gently undid the shackles and looked carefully at the sore on her leg. He applied something that stung and smelt very unpleasant.

"Not in great shape, are you? Maybe you need a bit more mothering, No Ma. We'll let Tara take charge of you."

Noma, as she was now called, was brought into the paddock, and the men stood around and watched. Tara was a full grown female elephant, but not as big as Noma's own mother. She had much smaller ears, and no tusks at all, but she seemed to be the acknowledged matriarch of the small group of elephants that lived in the compound.

Tara was aware of her audience, and she acted accordingly. She slowly approached the new elephant and touched her all over with her trunk. Noma stood still, quivering slightly with excitement. The other elephants stayed back, awaiting a cue from their leader. Tara held the stage, her trunk raised, briefly enjoying the attention. But the moment passed. She turned aside, ignoring the newcomer, and went back to munching her dinner. Slowly the others followed and, backs turned, resumed their interrupted meal.

"Well, no hostility at least. They should be fine in a day or two," said the man in the white coat. The men dispersed about their business, and Noma was left standing all alone by the gate.

The elephants were not fine in a day or two. Tara had recently been challenged in her dominion by another newly acquired elephant, and her honour had been saved only by the timely sale of her rival to another outfit. She was not going to allow that to happen again. At every opportunity, when the men were not around, she butted, slapped, and kicked her new charge. The other elephants, all Indians imported for work in the forest industry, followed Tara's lead. They shunned Noma most of the time and shoved her out of the way if she tried to join them.

After some weeks, when the men assumed she had settled in, they started to train Noma for work. The elephants were used to lift and carry trees that fell in difficult areas where machines couldn't get in to harvest them. Each had a trainer who guided his own animal and gave it instructions. Noma's trainer was an old man whose last elephant had died. He missed his old friend and didn't consider Noma worthy of his talents. He had little patience with her ignorance and ineptitude, and he beat her when she dropped the log he gave her, or stumbled in the brush.

"With ears that big, you'd think you could hear what I'm saying, you little runt. Get over there! Go, go, go!"

There was no trust between them, and no encouragement or sympathy for Noma in the eyes of the other elephants. The trainer reported that he was getting nowhere with her and finally quit elephant work all together. No-one else wanted to take her on. Bill was already regretting his apparent bargain and looking for buyers. Only the man in the white coat had any time for her. He fussed over the open sore on her leg, and he finally got it to heal over. But even he didn't see the deeper, underlying wound.

Within the year, Bill had found a buyer. A rather shabby caravan of trucks came by, carrying cages of various sized animals, from lions to lemurs, and stopped to buy feed from the farm side of the business. The owner happened to be looking for a replacement elephant for his menagerie, and Bill persuaded him that young Noma, so small and docile, would be a good investment. A hard bargain was struck, but both men were relieved to have solved their problems.

* * *

The next period of her life was an endless blur to Noma. She spent her nights and half her days tethered to a steel post, wherever the travelling zoo set up camp. Occasionally she would be led around a ring or along a street as part of a parade, with crowds of faces, young and old, laughing or cheering or staring at her. The eyes were always distant, alien, uninvolved.

The community of animals was restless and fearful. Predators crouched and watched with flicking tails, stalking in vain their nervous prey caged close by – an attempt to please the crowd with a parody of natural ecology. The elephant was neither hunted nor hunter. Alone in her well of misery, she bided her time.

After many years travelling up and down the continent, changing hands a few times, Noma found herself in a big sea port. The sounds and smells were different: deep horns blowing, engines chugging, yells, thuds, splitting plywood, newly dyed cloth, water lapping and lurching, fruit rotting, dust and litter clogging, sweet blossom, gas fumes, sullen heat turning fresh and salty in the early evening. She was penned in a yard alongside patched and shambled warehouses, away from the oil storage tanks and passenger liners. Her neighbour was an older elephant with a fine growth of tusks, who showed some interest in her, but their trunks barely touched over the barrier. Noma's own tusks were hardly yet visible.

Three men came over to inspect them one day, and Noma's neighbour was the main focus.

"She looks a good bet. Know any tricks? Good temperament?"

The elephant trader was quick to praise his prize specimen and gave a glowing report.

"Of course, you'd want the tusks taken off for a circus performer. I could do that for you, no trouble. She'd be ready to ship in about a week."

"I expect a discount for the ivory. I'm sure you can find a use for it. As you know, I'm not allowed to import it."

The deal was sealed, and the new owner drove off towards the airport. The trader turned to his assistant.

"Don't touch that one; I've another buyer lined up who'll pay bigger bucks. And a bonus for the tusks intact. Give it a couple of weeks, then crate up that other bunch of skin 'n bones and ship it off. By the time it arrives and the complaints roll in, this one 'll be long gone, no trace. We'll say it was a bad voyage, the animal got sick or whatever. He won't be able to prove any different, stupid sod."

And so Noma set out on her longest journey yet, to a country unknown, over seas rougher than any road, and this time even her identity was left behind.

* * *

The new world which greeted the elephant on a frosty November morning, with a leaden sun hanging just above the horizon, was no more welcoming than the one she had left. Weary crewmen prodded her down the gangplank into yet another trailer, and she was driven off to join the circus. She took the full brunt of the new owner's anger at the deception and was lucky not to end up in the knacker's yard. One quiet voice spoke up for her, the owner's son.

"Dad, she's not that bad. I could handle her, I'm sure. I've always wanted to train my own animal."

As once before, the son prevailed on the father, and the elephant was led off to a tiny yard behind the trailers, cages, canvas, and machinery. She huddled in a corner, biding her time, expecting to be either ignored or abused. The young man, small and skinny like herself, with tawny brown eyes, came and sat near her every morning before breakfast and again in the afternoon, when he had finished his chores. He didn't speak, just read a book or wrote notes, but she found herself waiting for him to come every day. He would take peanuts or other treats out of his pocket and put them down on the bench beside him. She snuffled them up after he had left.

Then one day he began murmuring softly to himself, and she strained forward to catch the tenor of his words, brushing his shoulder with her trunk. He looked at her then, smiled, and greeted her for the first time.

"Do you think we could be friends, Zoë? I hope you like that name. I have no idea what name you are used to – there is nothing in your papers. The vet says that you have probably had a rough life so far and you need feeding up, so I am not going to hurry you. But maybe one day you would like to perform with me? My name is Cas, by the way."

The elephant liked the sound of this voice, and she would touch the man's shoulder every day when he came, just to make him talk to her. She accepted the treats he gave her whenever she did this. Training began before she had realized it. The man started walking around the yard while he talked to her, and she followed, both to hear his voice and to get a treat. When he changed direction, so did she. He would pick up objects and hand them to her – skittles, balls, flags. Sometimes he would juggle with them first and throw her one, which she learned to catch with her trunk. Sometimes he did somersaults and walked on his hands, which confused her at first, but she got used to it. Another day, he lifted her front leg and put it onto a stool. Then he climbed up and sat on her neck, with his feet rubbing the backs of her ears. It was a very strange sensation, but he didn't stay there long, and after a few days she got used to this also. Then he started to do handstands, forward rolls, backflips, and split jumps along her back, and even juggled upside down with his head on top of hers, and she caught the skittles when he dropped them. He tried a few times to get her to stand on a small drum platform, but as she was obviously uncomfortable, he did not insist.

"Here, give her a prod with this," called one of the other circus men, watching with amusement. He threw a short metal rod over to Cas, who looked at it with disgust.

"I don't need a shock stick, thank you. Everything this elephant does is going to be her choice. I won't trust my life to an animal that's been goaded or beaten into submission."

"Suit y'self, laddie. But your Dad's expecting a show soon. He can't go on feeding a lazy bag o' bones for no return."

"We'll be ready, Mac, don't worry. And at least this act doesn't need steel cages and sharpshooters to keep the audience safe. One of these days, those tigers are going to pluck up the courage to bite you back."

Cas's first show was staged a couple of weeks later, as a warm up for the big acts. Zoë was nervous of the crowd at first, but when she concentrated on Cas and followed his lead, she was fine. The performance was rated a success, and the elephant's future was now a lot more secure.

The trust between elephant and man grew stronger as the months and years passed, and the act developed into a major showcase for the circus, a demonstration of the natural affinity and friendship between man and animal. The tiger act was downgraded and finally eliminated by the problems of expense and animal rights' activists.

One of the highlights of the elephant show was when Zoë was blindfolded and led around the ring, where Cas lay in her path, gagged and bound. With infinite delicacy, she sensed where he lay and stepped over him, lifting one foot at a time, without even nudging him. The crowd always clenched, gasped, and then cheered at this feat.

The circus pulled into the capital city one night, with a full parade and advance publicity. A royal command show was planned, with many celebrity guests. There was extra spit and polishing, laundering, rehearsing, sweeping, and grooming, and the excitement fermented into a froth of balloons, clowns, drums, spandex, and sparkles. Zoë kept her gaze steadily on Cas and followed him into the ring as the band played their fanfare. The performance was going well, when the Ringmaster stepped into the spotlight.

"Ladies and gentlemen! A big cheer for Caspar and Zoë! . . . And now I have a special announcement. We welcome here today the world famous Safari guide, philanthropist, and animal conservationist – Arnulf Henshaw!

"Thank you . . . Thank you, ladies and gentlemen. Mr. Henshaw has been so impressed by this act that he has volunteered to put his very own life in the hands of this remarkable trainer and his elephant! He will allow himself to be bound and gagged for the famous finale, in which the elephant will walk over him!"

The spotlight swung into the audience, where a tall man slowly stood up and bowed in all directions. People made way for him to reach the front, where he climbed over the boards and into the ring. His piercing green eyes rested briefly on the elephant, and then he limped over to where Cas was preparing the bonds.

Time stood still. The crowd vanished into mist, and blood surged and pounded in the elephant's ears. Her life unravelled before her as she watched the handcuffs and leg shackles being fitted, the silk scarf knotted behind his head. She felt her mother's rage, heard the shots ring out, and the dying scream. She had bided her time, and now the moment, unlooked for, barely hoped for, had come.

The Ringmaster helped Cas place the black velvet hood over Zoë's head and muttered "Make this look good, Cas. We paid that git big money for this stunt. Your father's counting on you. Good luck!"

Cas pulled gently on her ear and whispered, "OK, Zoë, let's do it. Just the same as usual, only a different body. Let's give them a show."

The elephant walked slowly round the ring, sweeping the sand with her trunk, seeking the faint scent, a breath, a twitch, the presence of her prey. She trembled as she caught it. She raised her front foot and nicely judged the distance to the centre of the soft belly.

"That's it. Good girl. Easy does it," came the soft reassurance from Cas. Loving. Caring. The only creature in the last twenty years who had shown her any value in life, any respect. He trusted her, and she had brought him value and respect in turn. But now she could bring him pain, anger, and shame. She no longer cared about these things for herself, but for him? . . .

The elephant made her choice, but the hesitation had upset her balance. Her back leg, still weak after all these years, gave way. She stumbled forward onto her knees, crushing the bound man. The velvet hood fell off, and she saw terror in the green eyes, bewilderment in the brown eyes, before Mac and his sharpshooter raised their guns. Two shots rang out. The world was torn apart, and the elephant bided her time no more.

The End

Maiden Grimm

My sister was more daring than I was. Of course, she was five years' older and knew I looked up to her. And she listened to what the grown-ups talked about, while I lived in a wonderland of fairy princesses, wicked witches, and one-eyed ogres.

This June morning was a perfect day for adventuring. We set out across the sheep pasture, giving the ram a wide berth, and as soon as we were out of sight of the farmhouse, we cut across to the road. We hung on the gate for a few minutes, listening intently for sounds of cars or horses coming down the lane, and then scampered across. We were soon hidden in the wood, picking our way through the lush summer growth of dog's mercury, nettles, and clumps of foxgloves. On the other side of the wood we stood in the shelter of the trees and looked out on the ramshackle orchard that had once been an active part of the farm.

The tinker's wooden shack, patched with torn shingles, stood glowering at us from among the old gnarled apple trees, which now carried garlands of wild rose blossom from the briars entwined round their trunks. We crept forward, and my sister carefully untied the string and lifted the door latch. I felt like Goldilocks. There was an old table with a plate, bowl, and mug, and a chair with a broken cane back. On the back wall was a shabby couch covered with a rug and misshapen cushions, and on a small chest in the corner stood a wash basin and dented tin kettle. A grimy camp stove made up the kitchen, together with a couple of shelves holding soap, pans, matches, a candle stub, some tins of soup, tea, and an open packet of stale biscuits.

"Let's light the stove and make some tea," my sister said. Not quite a whisper, but enough for me to know she was not entirely at ease.

"Are you sure he's gone?" I whispered back.

"They said he wouldn't be back till pea-picking time. He's on his travels at the moment."

She spoke a little louder this time. I sat on the chair, which was too hard, and then on the bed, which was lumpy and covered with white cat hairs. My sister was fiddling with the stove, trying to remember her Brownie camp-lore. We both heard the gate at the other end of the orchard creak as it swung open. We stared at each other for a few petrified seconds. Then we scrambled for the door and fled back into the wood as fast as our legs could carry us.

* * *

In Sunday School we learned about the Good Samaritan. Our teacher, Miss Lawrence, was very keen on making us real Christians rather than just memorizing bible verses, so she said we should all go home and think about someone who was overlooked or avoided by everyone else. And then we should help that person in some way and tell the class about what we had done next Sunday, when the Rector would be inspecting us. I think she wanted to impress the Rector, who was young and trendy and gave sermons that the old ladies in the Post Office muttered darkly about.

My Mum suggested I make some gingerbread and take it down to Granny Beazley, who lived in an old thatched cottage the other side of our wood. She was a little peppery, and not quite in her right mind some days, which was why people tended to avoid her.

"She's harmless enough, and I think she would fit your project perfectly."

With Mum's help, I baked some gingerbread men, wrapped them in a tea towel, and tied them with some ribbon. I got out my bike, popped the package in the basket on the front, and set out carefully down the road.

The wood lay on my right, a colourful patchwork of autumn reds, yellows and oranges, the dry leaves rustling gently. I noticed the barbed wire which ran along the other side of the ditch. Last year my Dad had fenced off this bit of woodland to allow the farm boar to roam freely. It was a monstrous creature, with tusks and a bad temper, and it wasn't safe to wander in there anymore. I continued down the road till I got to the end of the fencing, where a grassy track led through the wood towards the old orchard. Granny Beazley's cottage was on the other side, a bit further down the road, but I stopped my bike here and did some thinking. My Mum might consider Granny Beazley harmless, but a few months ago she had caught me crawling through her hedge to steal her strawberries. She had given me quite a scare, shaking her old broom at me and threatening to skin me alive if she saw me anywhere near her property again. I hadn't told my Mum about that, for obvious reasons. No, I didn't want to risk knocking on her door in case she remembered me.

I looked up the track. I could hear someone chopping logs somewhere over the brier hedge. The old tinker's shack lay up there. My sister and I had been there once when I was much younger, and it was like the pictures of African shanty huts in the missionary books. I was sure no-one ever did nice things for the tinker, or he wouldn't live in such a hovel. I pulled my bike off the road, hid it behind the hedge, took out the package of gingerbread men, and set off up the track. I wasn't at all afraid this time as I skipped along.

He looked at me in a funny way when he opened the door and I told him why I was there.

"I want to help make you happy because no-one else cares about you, but I do, and Miss Lawrence said I had to, because it's what Jesus wants us to do, so I have made these for you. My Mum meant me to take them to Granny Beazley, but I don't like her and I think you deserve them much more. No-one will know I changed my mind. Granny B.'s a bit do-lally anyway, she won't remember if I was there or not, so it will be our secret."

He didn't even glance at the gingerbread, though I had wrapped it up really prettily. He beckoned me in and said he'd be back in a moment. I sat on the lumpy bed and stroked his cat for a while. Then I looked round, and he was standing in the doorway with all his clothes off. His body was all white and soft apart from his grimy hands and his face and neck, which were sunburnt and leathery. Except for the big red thing he was pointing at me. He told me what he wanted me to do to help make him happy. I took a deep breath and remembered what Miss Lawrence had said. And then I was a Good Samaritan.

Next Sunday I told Miss Lawrence and the Rector that I had taken gingerbread men to Granny Beazley. They said very good, we hope you'll keep it up, and gave me an extra big sticker for my Sunday School book. After that I was a Good Samaritan almost every week, and at the end of the term I graduated to the next class with a full book.

* * *

When I was twelve my parents sent me away to boarding school. I didn't want to go. The year before, I had managed to fail the eleven-plus exam that would have qualified me for the county grammar school, and so I stayed on at the friendly village all-grade school. But to no avail. My parents said they were prepared to make sacrifices so I would get a better education and a brighter future at a private institution. I submitted to the dull, grey, box pleated skirts, stiff-collared blouses, tie, straw boater, ankle length gabardine raincoat, and everything else three sizes too big (to allow for growth). I looked ridiculous, but I fitted right in with the other new girls.

We all compared and shared our life experience and secret knowledge at night in the dormitory, which didn't really amount to much beyond rumour and wishful thinking. I didn't tell anyone about the tinker, as that seemed quite outside anyone else's range of facts or fantasies, and I didn't want to appear odd. That all changed when we started hygiene lessons.

At first we learned to wash our hands after going to the toilet, to brush our teeth while counting to fifty, and to always carry a sanitary napkin and safety pins. After cleanliness and health care came sex. And this was a revelation to us all.

The textbook picture of male genitals bore no resemblance to the body of the tinker. There was no thick rug of hair, and the penis hung down, meek and insignificant, with tubes and sacs superimposed on the drawing to show the mechanics of insemination. None of the girls believed that such a paltry organ could possibly perform the feats described by the gym mistress, who was responsible for these classes, but no-one dared challenge her grim-faced presentation.

Afterwards, in the giggly blackness of the boarding house bedrooms, the lessons were dissected at length, and I could no longer resist contributing my unique piece of knowledge. No-one was quite sure if I was boasting or kidding, but as I was normally quiet and conventional, I was gradually given the benefit of the doubt. What I described of the tinker's anatomy, and what I had done with it, was not part of the curriculum and therefore all the more fascinating. We speculated for hours on whether or not I could be pregnant (I had not yet started my periods) and on whether the tinker's organ, not to mention my own, would perform in textbook fashion. Swept up on this wave of intense admiration and interest, I promised to find out in the school holidays.

* * *

It was after Christmas before I had a chance to follow up my research, and I waited until the rest of the family went into town for the Boxing Day sales before venturing down to the orchard. I hadn't visited for several years, and he was surprised, and a little wary, to see me. I had brought some Christmas cake with me, which he ate, and then I told him about our hygiene classes. I said I didn't think we had been doing it right, according to our book, and perhaps he could help me work it out. I don't think he was that keen at first, but when I took my skirt and knickers off and started hauling up my sweater, he got quite red and fidgety. By the time I had all my clothes off he was struggling with his belt and buttons, and his organ sprang out, fully justifying my description of it. (I had wondered, when telling my tale, if I had exaggerated.)

What happened next is a bit of a blur. I had intended to go through the procedure slowly to check the facts, but I was pushed roughly down on the couch, my legs thrown up and wide apart, and then he was slobbering and biting all over my bottom and right between my legs. I could feel a flush spreading up my body and a weird kind of excitement, and then a jabbing, searing pain as he rammed his hot poker tightly into my bruised and burning flesh. He shuddered a few times, and I felt the fire go out of him. I lay there shivering as the slime dripped down my thighs and settled in an icy puddle under my bottom. He was already buttoning up his trousers again and, thrusting a dirty towel at me, he told me gruffly to clean myself up and get out.

I could barely stumble my way back home through the wood and across the fields, I was aching and trembling so much. I ran a hot bath and had managed to recover some of my composure by the time the family got home. I told my mother I was still recovering from my headache and went to bed early. She thought I was getting my first period.

I never did get my first period. Several months later, I was taken out of boarding school and sent to a private nursing home on the south coast, and I had no more contact with the girls at school, people in the village, the tinker, or even my own father. Hedged in by nurses, nuns, and the quiet cocoon of books, I surrendered myself to their tranquil charm.

* * *

The sister in charge of the home was an elderly nun, and she used to come to my room almost every evening to see how I was and help me get to bed. She loved to brush my hair for me. I had been growing it since I was nine, and I could almost sit on it. My mother wanted me to cut it off for boarding school, as the regulations didn't allow hair to touch your shoulders, but I kept it bound up in plaits across my head. Sister Mary Magdalene told me it was beautiful and that I should take good care of it. I asked her if she had long hair too – you couldn't see behind all that veil and drapery – but she sighed and said she had cut it all off a long time ago when she became a bride of Christ. As time went on, she did more than just brush my hair, but I didn't like to say anything. She was a nun after all. I had already been warned about my wicked thoughts and fantasies leading me astray.

It was hot that June, and in the afternoons, when I was supposed to be doing my school work, I would open the windows wide and lean out, letting my hair float down in the warm breeze. One afternoon I was startled to hear a voice speaking quietly from the shadows.

"I love the way your hair catches the sun."

I was very shy at first, but Richard did all the talking. He told me he was employed by the home to help in the garden during the summer as he lived nearby, but really he was a student at Kings College in London, studying Classics. On the third afternoon, he asked if he could come up to my room, as he was getting a crick in his neck and he wanted to see me properly. He climbed very nimbly up the rose trellis, and I helped him over the sill and into my room.

He had the most beautiful blue eyes and a strong young body, and I fell head over heels in love with him. When he held my hand I trembled. When he came close and put his arm round my shoulder, I nearly fainted. I longed for him to kiss my lips, to caress my breasts, to still the fluttering desire he had awakened in me, body and soul. This was what the poets wrote about, what star-crossed lovers defied and died for in our dusty, dog-eared textbooks. Those classic stories suddenly came alive for me, and the Harlequin romances we had devoured under the bedclothes by flashlight floated out the window like soap bubbles.

He was so gentle and unassuming. At first we sat on my bed and talked, holding hands. But after a week, I found this was such sweet torture that I plucked up courage to lift his hand and place it over my breast, my nipple hardening in expectation. Still he hesitated, but when I sighed and leaned against him, he smiled. With infinite care and patience, he began to undress me, covering each area of exposed skin with soft kisses and murmurs of admiration, even the growing bump of my tummy. By the time we were lying naked on my bed, bathed in the warm glow of the late afternoon sun, I was as ripe and ready to pluck as the golden apples of the Hesperides.

The summer wore on, and as we lay in each others' arms every afternoon, we made plans for the future, or at least I did. In my version, he would help me climb down the trellis at night, after Sister Mary Magdalene had seen me to bed, and we would catch a train to London and set up house together. He would finish his studies while I got a job, and then we'd go and live on a farm somewhere in the north where no-one would ever find us. I don't know whether he really believed any of this, but he smiled and kissed the tip of my nose and never said a word.

This magical summer ended with a thunderstorm that rivalled the wrath of the gods, but not the fury of Sister Mary Magdalene. The night that it broke, Richard and I had arranged a midnight tryst and a rehearsal of my escape. The evening became very still and heavy. Just after eleven, the first flickers appeared, and then came a regular, shuddering boom and hiss of blundering, bloated clouds. I buried my head in the pillows. When I felt the soft caress on my hair, I reached my hand over my shoulder to find his, whispering his name and a string of endearments. I was suddenly shaken and pulled up by my hair. Sister Mary Magdalene demanded to know who Richard was, and why was I expecting him. I foolishly blurted out my story, and her eyes blazed.

"You have been given every chance to redeem yourself here, you wicked slut! We have protected you and cared for you, and you have abused our trust and our love. You will pay for this!"

Then she took up the scissors from my table and cut off all my hair in great uneven chunks. I sobbed and cringed while she harangued me, until, her passion spent, she led me away to spend the night in her room on a camp bed, under her watchful eye. The very next day I was packed off, bag and baggage, to a big gloomy hospital with bars on the windows, somewhere in the wilds of Yorkshire, and I will never see my true love again.

* * *

Nobody believes me. I have been shut up in this little room for weeks now, and the doctor comes to see me every day and asks the same old questions. Like why did I cut off my hair. Sister

Mary Magdalene has not yet confessed to her venal sins. She might find it awkward to explain her fit of violent temper and jealousy, especially as Richard wasn't even there. I don't think she's mentioned him to anyone else, and nor will I. I don't want his name mixed up in all this trouble. I want to remember our summer together as the happiest time of my life. But if I could only come up with the name of the tinker, people might believe my story, and everything could turn out all right.

My sister claims she doesn't remember ever trespassing in the orchard or breaking into the tinker's shack, and my father said the man hasn't been seen in the village for several years. He certainly wasn't around last Christmas. Well, I'm not surprised if he did a quick bunk after my little visit to him – it obviously upset him. And he had only been back a couple of days then, and no-one but me had seen him. I think the headmistress and the nuns all thought my father was responsible. They kept encouraging me to blame it all on him, but that's nonsense. I mean, I have to do what he says, and he scares me sometimes, but he would never do anything like that, not my own father. They wouldn't even let him see me after they sent me away. Maybe that's just as well, as he is furious with me for letting him down, after he had boasted to everyone about the fancy school I was attending and that I had a great future ahead of me.

The girls at school didn't tell anyone about the tinker either. It's a sort of code of honour not to tell anything that's talked about in the dormitory. I couldn't expect them to break their honour. They were even afraid to come too close to me, after I told them what had happened at Christmas. They were scared it might be catching.

My baby is due any time now, the doctor says. But I won't be allowed to keep it if I can't tell them who the father is. Babies with no fathers get sent to the orphanage for adoption. It's hard to believe that's true today, in 1959; it sounds more like Oliver Twist or Jane Eyre. But that's what the doctor tells me, so I'm trying desperately to think of the tinker's name. I'm sure I heard him say it once. Was it Alex, Alan, Andy? Brendan, Bernie? I must write down all the names I can think of, and I will surely find the right one in the end.

~~Charlie~~	~~Gerald~~	~~Louis~~	~~Roald~~
~~Carlos~~	~~Harold~~	~~Morris~~	~~Roland~~
~~Carroll~~	~~Jerrold~~	~~Norris~~	~~Solomon~~
~~Darryl~~	~~Jakob~~	~~Norman~~	~~Tollman~~
~~Dan~~	~~Hansel~~	~~Orwell~~	~~Wallace~~
~~Evan~~	~~Henry~~	~~Powell~~	~~Wilhelm~~
~~Frederick~~	~~Ken~~	~~Paulo~~	
~~Garrick~~	~~Len~~	~~Raoul~~	

The End

Collision Course

Elfreda stood in front of her mirror, adjusting the red-brimmed hat with the dyed feathers. She was going with red today, rather than mustard, even though she had been told yellow was more visible to traffic. Her red winter coat was buttoned up to the neck and the scarf tucked in. Almost ready. She rummaged through the closet for her scuffed leather shopping bag and checked the contents: coin purse, candy canes, gloves, iron key, handkerchief, and tambourine. Better take the horn as well, in case of coyotes. She let herself out the back door, crept past the living room in case her new daughter-in-law was in there, and strode off up the hill.

* * *

Mrs. Penney fussed over her boy, Timmy, wiping a smear of butter off his face, and poured him a second cup of hot strong tea.

"Are you sure you don't want another egg, Timmy? It's no trouble."

"No. I don't want. Time for my bike."

Timmy fidgeted in his chair till his mother sighed and conceded defeat. However else she may have failed her son, she had always tried to keep his plate filled. Ramming his Chevy cap on backwards, Timmy ran outside to fetch his five-speed from the shed. He turned on the radio in the front carrier to full blast as he wheeled it down the drive. He carefully mounted and set off down the road, as he had done every morning, weather permitting, for the last thirty years.

* * *

Wayne Butler woke up, crouched in a basement stairwell. His head was fuzzy and his mouth felt like the bottom of a gravel truck. Ouch! Something was digging into his leg. He yanked his dad's old hunting knife out of his pocket. What was he carrying that around for? Through the fog in his brain, the events of last night began to emerge: getting drunk on George Street, buying some pills off a guy in the bar, showing off to that girl, his buddy daring him to . . . Oh Christ! He hadn't, had he? From his other pocket he pulled out a wooly balaclava, and a fistful of twenty dollar bills. God Almighty, had he actually walked into that corner store and robbed it? He could remember standing outside, with Jerry egging him on, but then his mind was a blank. In spite of the warmth of the early sun, he broke out in a cold sweat. Then he realized this wasn't even his house.

* * *

Elfreda preferred to walk up the middle of the road, so no coyotes could ambush her from the ditch. The occasional car was a nuisance, but they knew her well enough to slow down and go round her. She waved regally at those she liked, and shook her tambourine at the ones she judged had cut it too fine. There was hardly a soul out this morning, probably still sleeping off their Friday night. She stopped to admire the whitewashed church perched above the ocean. It was an old friend: baptisms, Sunday school as student and teacher, her wedding day, her husband's funeral, all encompassed within its sturdy walls. In there, she felt more connected to her life than out in the crazy world of today.

She fished the heavy iron key out of her bag and walked up to the stained oak doors. Her grandfather had paid for those out of his sealing money one bountiful spring. She stepped inside and felt the peace wash over her. Tapping the tambourine almost in time, she raised her quivering voice in a hymn of praise and then yelled Amen! several times over, enjoying the echoes bouncing off the high timbers. She didn't notice the parson furtively peeking through a side window. As a young man, fresh out of divinity college, he was intimidated by his parishioner's demand for access to the church at all times, and he had surrendered the old key. Fortunately, he had another key to the vestry door, and he scuttled in to lock up after her every day, scared that his domain would fall victim to roaming vandals if left open.

* * *

Wayne limped across the road to his own house, saw the Harley belonging to his mom's boyfriend parked out front, and had a flash of inspiration. He had best lie low for a while, in case Jerry ratted on him and the law came looking. His Nan lived round the bay. She had always spoiled him as a kid, and she'd be sure to take him in, no questions asked. She had no truck with his mom now, anyway. He crept into the house, found the key, and slipped out again. He was shaking a bit, so he popped another couple of pills to shore up his courage. He nearly fell under the full weight of the machine as he knocked the prop out, but managed to get it upright. He flung his leg over, kicked the starter, and the beast roared into action. He fled down the street, round the corner, and headed for the highway.

* * *

Coming back down the hill from the church, Elfreda spotted the Professor out walking his doberman, Karl. She beamed and hurried towards him, blowing her horn to catch his attention. Dr. Morrison inwardly groaned at his bad timing. Elfreda had taken a shine to him the first time he visited the community to collect material for his folklore thesis. She had plied him with tales – morbid, romantic, tragic, libellous, ridiculous – about neighbours, ancestors, monsters, and ghosts. He was never sure quite what to believe, but he had mined them for some anecdotal nuggets, and for that he was grateful. He had settled in the village after getting tenure at the university, and now he was paying the price.

"Professor, have a candy cane," said Elfreda, marching across the road, rummaging in her bag. "Put them on your Christmas tree for the children."

"Elfreda, it's July."

"Nonsense! Here, take them." She tried to stuff them in his pocket. Karl snarled and half choked himself on the leash trying to get her. "That dog needs more exercise. You should set it on the coyotes, not old ladies."

"Hey, Freddy!" The yell was almost drowned out by the blaring rock music of Timmy's radio, as he wobbled up to them in the middle of the road. He made a grab for the candy canes.

"Stop that, you sleeveen! And don't call me Freddy. I'm Mrs. Butler to you." Elfreda shook her tambourine fiercely in Timmy's face, nearly knocking him off the bike, while Karl went crazy at the sight of the spinning spokes.

* * *

Off the highway into this bedlam came a motorbike doing 120 kph. Wayne swerved sharply around the group in the middle of the road and careened on round the corner, where he skidded on the gravel shoulder and struck a rock. He went head over heels, still astride the bike, over the guard rail, down the cliff, and into the deep water below.

* * *

Dr. Morrison managed to pull Elfreda away from Timmy, who was now laughing hysterically. He took the candy canes, gave one to Timmy, and beat a hasty retreat with Karl. Timmy rode away, sucking the candy cane, pleased with his little victory. Elfreda looked round, startled, suddenly aware that something strange had happened, then shrugged.

"Too much traffic," she muttered, "Someone could get killed." And she hurried on down the road after the Professor.

The End

Tabula Rasa

That was it then. Jimmy was gone. A lifetime of care finished with. Lillian stared at the old desk in the back room and picked at the scotch tape still adhering to the pitted wood, where countless sheets of newspaper had been taped down over the years. Jimmy loved to paint, in his extravagant way; water, brushes, paint pots, scattered all over the desk; and wet pieces of paper dripping with colours, bright and blurry. They were hard to keep. The paper went crinkly when it dried, and the paints cracked if you flattened it. Not that Jimmy minded. He lived always in the present.

She supposed Margaret would be here soon. She should have called her earlier, but it all happened so suddenly; the fall, the stroke, the frantic calls to the ambulance, the emergency room, the decisions to take. Margaret would be angry and upset and probably tell her off for trying to cope on her own, but what else was she to do if her daughter lived so far away?

Lillian wandered round the room, picking up objects and framing the memories: a piece of quartz that Jimmy called his frozen star; a scrapbook of pictures of movie stars, fashion models, and sports heroes; the chipped green mug with a porcelain frog in the bottom – his favourite, but impossibly difficult to clean; the photograph of his father (damn the bastard!) that he would never let her take down. She smoothed the rumpled sheet on the daybed and pulled the blanket over it. She could never get him to make his bed, she'd have to try some other . . . She sat down heavily and hugged the pillow to herself, before burying her face in it. The tears spurted. Smell was the most primitive, evocative, gut-wrenching of all the senses, and for a brief time she let it have full sway, weeping for all the tomorrows there would never be.

Margaret was taking her time. She should have been here by now. Maybe she was sulking again because she wasn't kept in the picture. She was always jealous of Jimmy, even when he was a baby, before they knew about his special needs. She'd have gone with Dave if he'd have taken her, but the courts didn't like that back then. Mothers got to keep the kids, dads just had to pay. She was the one who had to carry the burden, day in, day out, with no help from him, and Margaret under her feet as well.

Lillian went back to the desk and sat down. Her finger traced the pale water mark that flowed across the surface. She smiled. Jimmy had surprised her on her birthday once – funny that he remembered when it was – by giving her flowers.

He picked all the dandelions off the grass at the back of the house and stuck them in her prize crystal vase, the one her grandmother gave her. He must have knocked it against the tap, because it was chipped near the bottom, and leaked water all over the desk while he went looking for her. Margaret had mopped it up with the embroidered table runner that had taken Lillian months to complete. Stupid thing to do, she had told her she ought to know better. It quite spoiled the day, her cloth being ruined like that.

Where was she? It didn't take this long to drive into town. Never around when she was needed, Margaret, just like her father. The tears pricked behind her eyes again, but she rubbed them away. She was quite alone now. She couldn't be giving into fits of maudlin sentiment, even though the black hole in her heart threatened to devour her.

The door bell rang, and there were footsteps in the hall.

"Mom? Are you there?"

Lillian took a deep breath, patted her hair into place and got to her feet.

"I'm in the back, dear. Just straightening up a bit."

Margaret came into the room, took a quick glance round, and stepped awkwardly towards her mother. They exchanged a brief hug.

"So sorry about Jimmy, Mom. Are you all right?" They moved apart again. "I wish you'd called me sooner. I'm sorry I'm so late, but Ken is still out on a job, and I had to find a sitter for Jason, and then the car was low on gas, and I . . ."

Lillian had turned away, was staring out the window.

"It's OK, you don't need to make excuses. I know it's difficult, you have your own lives to live. Jimmy and I do just . . . we managed . . . just fine.

"But it would have been nice for you to have been here, to have come more often. You are his only sister, he didn't have anyone else, just me. It's hard sometimes, taking all that on by yourself."

Margaret reached out a hand to touch her mother's shoulder, but it was shrugged off.

"I . . . we . . . Look, I'm sorry about Jimmy, Mom. Really I am. I know it's been hard for you. But it wasn't easy, either, being his sister, trying to help him. He could be very . . . He wasn't always very . . . gentle. I was afraid to bring Jason here, to be honest. I worried –

"Don't be ridiculous, Margaret, he wouldn't have hurt a fly!"

Margaret flushed but stood her ground. "I didn't always tell you everything he did. He had quite a temper, you know he did."

They both glanced towards the old desk, where the side was gashed deeply and one drawer hung slightly askew, splinters missing. Silence hung between them like a still fog.

"Well, aren't you going to ask me what happened?" asked Lillian eventually, trying to clear the air. "After they gave up trying to save him, the doctors told me I had a decision to make. They wanted to study him. They said it helps them help others like Jimmy in the future. I had to give them an answer right away, while he . . . while the cells were fresh."

"Oh, Mom, that's awful! I didn't realize. You really should have called me, we could have talked about – "

"It doesn't matter, it was my decision." Lillian took another deep breath and bit her lip, looking away. "Anyway . . . what would you have done, Margaret?"

"Don't worry, Mom, I would have done exactly the same as you. Anything they can do to help prevent another tragedy like Jimmy . . ." Too late, Margaret realized her mistake. Her mother turned on her, white-faced, fists clenched.

"You're all the same, you and those doctors! You don't see Jimmy as a human being, who had every right to live, just like you and me. He wasn't some specimen to mess around with. I was the only one who cared for him. You and his father, you both hated him, you both resented him, but I loved him, he was my only son . . . " Lillian caught her breath in a sob and brought her fist to her mouth. She fought to keep control of herself, and after a few moments continued quietly, "I've arranged for the undertakers to pick him up today. He'll be cremated on Friday. I hope that's all right with you, won't interfere with your schedule?"

Margaret flushed again, but bit her tongue. She knew how hard this was for her mother, but she wished she wouldn't take it out on her. She was always so prickly where Jimmy was concerned, jumping to his defence, even when he had done something bad. As the healthy, normal, older sister she could never win. Lately, she had to admit, she had given up trying. Feeling the guilt, she went to give her mother another reassuring hug, but Lillian brushed past her and went through to the kitchen.

"I suppose you'd like a cup of tea now you're here?"

* * *

After the funeral, when the minister, neighbours, friends, and the nurse from the community daycare centre had finished nibbling the sandwiches and sipping the sherry, mother and daughter sat nursing cups of tea in the kitchen, taking comfort from the warmth in their hands. Lillian was exhausted after a week of busying herself with funeral details, and tidying and untidying the house as she tried to organize the bits and pieces of her unfinished life with Jimmy.

"I think you should take a little holiday, Mom." Margaret broke the fragile peace. "When I talked to cousin Ellen in Ontario, she sounded anxious to see you. It's been years, she said."

"She could always have come here if she wanted to see us."

"Yes, I know. But still, she has offered to have you and give you a break, so you can take it easy for a few weeks. I can clean up the house for you while you're away, and when you get back, we can talk about the future. Ken and I would be happy to have you live with us, and Jason would love to see more of his grandmother. You have tended to neglect him, you know, and he's a lovely, bright little boy. Ken has been doing up the basement, and we could easily turn it into a self-contained apartment for you. You could – "

"We'll have to see, dear. I can't think about any of this now."

"Well, shall I call Ellen? When would you like to go?"

"I don't know, I'm just so tired."

"Leave it to me, then. I'll book a ticket. I'm sure it's for the best, getting away for a while. I'll take care of things this end."

* * *

When Lillian returned to her house a month later, she had to admit it looked very smart. The paint work was clean, the yard neat and tidy, the air in the hall fresh and lightly scented. Margaret had done a good job. Lillian could never fault her on her housework. She wandered through into the back room, while Ken took her suitcase upstairs.

A single white rose bloomed perfectly in a slender glass stem vase, in the middle of an embroidered cloth on the desk. Next to it, a framed photograph of a teenage boy, with carefully combed hair and clean white shirt and tie, stared at her across the room. Lillian grasped a chair and sat down.

"Happy Birthday, Mom. I hope you like it." Margaret had followed her mother into the room, Jason peeking out from behind her skirt.

"But where . . . ?"

"It's a copy of that cloth you embroidered years ago, the one that was spoiled. I found the pattern when I was clearing out and thought I'd make you another."

"But the photograph, I've never seen that before."

Margaret looked sheepish. "Dad had it taken that time you were in hospital and Jimmy was put in care. We took him out for the day. But Jimmy hated that picture, wouldn't let us give it you – you know how stubborn he was. We didn't insist, he got so agitated. But I kept a copy."

The eyes in the photograph spoke of betrayal and infinite sadness, in the poor deformed face she hardly recognised as her own son, so neat and clean was it, all animation suspended.

"And see what Ken has done, Mom." Margaret was flustered with anticipation as she moved the vase and picture to one side and folded up the cloth. Gleaming wood, satin finished without a scratch or stain, was revealed. The sides were perfectly straight and unnotched, the drawers hung evenly, the patched splinters barely showing beneath several coats of tawny varnish.

"Mom, don't you think it looks great? I bet it wasn't in this good shape when you bought it for Jimmy all those years ago."

Lillian sat stock still, while her world went giddy around her. She had managed to pull herself together at Ellen's, resolved to try and move on, give Margaret and her family a chance, but now . . . Not only had she lost all her tomorrows with Jimmy, but as the tears coursed down her face unchecked, she realized that all the yesterdays had also been completely, irredeemably, erased.

The End

Miracle Boy

At ten o'clock on a chill November morning in 1974, a man walked into the Harrison Memorial Stadium in Trunkie Bay, Newfoundland, with three hand guns and a semi-automatic and mowed down a class of five year olds, as they slid, skated, and staggered around on the ice with their young teacher and two parent assistants. The incident took less than five minutes. Before one of the parents could drag her shattered leg to the telephone on the wall, the man put the last gun to his own head and shot off half his face. It took a little longer for the blood to seep through the snowsuits and winter jackets, spreading scarlet stains across the ice among the prostate bodies with their white safety helmets. Twelve children and the teacher died instantly. Three of five in critical condition died later that day, and two others suffered flesh wounds, with splintered bones or deep cuts. In the middle of the bloody carnage stood Philip Greene, small for his five and a half years, still balanced on his skates, and not a bruise or a scratch on him.

Trunkie Bay is one of a string of small towns off the Trans-Canada highway in eastern

Newfoundland, their backs to the road and their kitchen doors and living rooms open to the sea. The shock wave spread from the arena in ever widening circles through these communities, and like an echo, it drew circles of cars, onlookers, families, and parents, following the sirens of police and ambulance. The yellow tape was already in place, cordoning off the gravel car park around the squat rectangular building, when Philip's mother arrived.

In silence broken only by the occasional sob and the whimpering of a small baby, the bodies were brought out one by one, huddled under blankets, barely filling half a stretcher each. A helicopter rose in a flurry of haste, tearing into the wind to reach the hospital in St. John's with its cargo of survivors. A policeman was consulting in low tones with the school principal, who clutched a piece of paper in his shaking hand, checking off names. But it didn't need a list to spot the blanched faces, rigid with shock and horror, of the parents of the Kindergarten class.

Mrs. Greene was getting close to the point of hysteria by the time the principal was escorting the policeman from one wretched parent to the next, leaving a wake of clustering family and neighbours around each shattered life. And then a small solemn figure appeared from the back of the arena, a policewoman guiding him forward and looking anxiously for a sign of recognition. Mrs. Greene screamed "Philip! Sweet Jesus, Philip!" and thrust her way through the murmuring crowd, under the tape, to gather her son into her ample arms. And the tears she wept were of pure relief and joy, mingling with the bitter, wrenching sobs of her neighbours.

As reports of the senseless tragedy hummed along the news wires and were broadcast to the world, the global village gathered round to stare and mourn and voice its opinions vicariously through the media. St. John's airport was suddenly thick with in-coming flights, and taxi companies, car rental firms, and local hotels made a quick bonus as reporters flocked to the scene.

It was important to the press to get a good angle on the story, something that would rivet the attention beyond the sheer horror of the age and number of the slaughtered. They all tried, but it was difficult. The police were as yet uncertain of the identity and motives of the murderer, and they kept tight-lipped about how the man had managed to acquire so much weaponry. Families of the dead children quickly closed ranks against the probing into their misery, after witnessing one father openly sobbing and clinging to his wife, purging his own guilt and pain, and that of the whole community, before the relentless cameras. A request was made by the town council to respect the privacy of the funeral rites, and indeed the Wesleyan chapel and Salvation Army citadel could barely cope with just the friends and families of each young victim. The graveyards exhibited unnatural gaiety, with carpets of flowers day after day, though they quickly withered in the cruel night frosts and freezing drizzle.

In desperation, one local reporter had scanned the list of names of the Kindergarten class, obtained from one of the teachers in the confusion of the first day, and called up every family. Of those who had not already taken their phones off the hook, most had a family spokesperson to field the calls, and his requests were firmly, and not always politely, refused. But when he dialled up the Greene household, he was overwhelmed by the bubbling joy of the mother who answered and was still thanking God for her son's deliverance.

"It was a miracle, sir, a blessed miracle! My Philip is the luckiest boy alive. I feel he has been chosen, sir, he's special. Not a scratch on him, he just stood there and never even lost his balance. What a saint!"

The story was there. He scribbled a few notes and ran out to the news room. One of the copy editors was explaining over the phone to a reporter in Toronto how Trunkie Bay got its name: from a corruption of the French 'Baie Tranquille'. Not much of an angle, but amusing to mainlanders. The whole news room was excited by the news of a mother willing to talk, and in no time the headlines were appearing all over North American supermarkets. "Miracle Boy Survives Slaughter!" "Mother Claims Son a Saint!" "Miracle in Trunkie Bay!" Miracle was the keyword, and even the higher class papers took up the story, and TV cameras again descended on the little town. A ray of light in an otherwise unbearable tragedy was what the world wanted, something meaningful to fasten on to in the face of chaos. The suicide murderer had now been identified as an unemployed electrician from a neighbouring town, who had just returned from the States. He was a quiet man with no history of violence, divorced with two small children who were in his wife's custody. They were not among the victims but were being shielded by the police. He had no other close relatives or friends who could account for his act of madness, but he was known to have collected *Soldier of Fortune* magazines. His name would join the growing ranks of the quiet loners who have snatched notoriety from the jaws of death.

* * *

The flowers and cards, which had been sent by the hundreds to the little town in its first days of mourning, were now replaced by cheques and pledges and dollar bills in scruffy envelopes by the thousands, to set up a fund for the survivors of the tragedy. The little ray of light, otherwise known as Philip Greene, had sparked the fires of charity in the hearts of people world-wide, seeking to ward off the evil-eye of pitiless savagery which invaded their living rooms. The fund was administered by one of the big banks in St. John's, as it was really too large a sum to be left in the hands of the municipal council or any of the local service clubs. It was registered as the Philip Greene Fund, partly because his name was almost always mentioned in the letters, and even on the cheques, but also because his solemn young face was a marketing executive's dream logo. Not that the fund was deliberately promoted, but its growth was regularly monitored by the media, professors of anthropology, and other interested parties. After a year or so, however, the donations had dried up. Soon, public outrage would be redirected to another form of Newfoundland brutality. The baby seal hunt drew a far greater flow of money to the highly marketed funds of various animal welfare groups, who had found an even more appealing logo in the soulful eyes of a fluffy seal pup, portrayed against a similar background of blood on the ice.

* * *

It is difficult to pinpoint when the hostility towards Philip Greene began to emerge. At first everyone in Trunkie Bay was happy that at least one little boy had survived the massacre unscathed, and they indulged his mother's unabated joy with tolerant understanding. The grieving families were glad to have the pressure of attention removed from themselves. Many were impressed by the donations which poured in, and they were grateful for this mark of humanity which had been so lacking in the crime. The first few cheques had been distributed to the most needy families to help defray funeral expenses, for the community wanted no distinctions made between those who could afford the whole paraphernalia and those who couldn't. As more money came, and the Miracle Boy story gained prominence, a well-meaning local politician had expressed concerns about the proper use of the fund, to safeguard the future education and welfare of Philip Greene and the other four surviving children. The bank stepped in and set up a legal trust. From then on, formal application had to be made to the trustees to release any monies, and proper accounting for it submitted. Most families turned their backs on it, but continued to accept the help and support of their neighbours. Newfoundland outports had a long tradition of self help and cooperation in their isolated history.

The Kindergarten class did not get a replacement teacher. The school board could not justify the expense for so few children. Philip was the only one who returned to school before Christmas, a photo opportunity in his Sunday best clothes, neat little satchel, and demurely lowered eyes. He was slotted into the Grade One section for the time being, where no-one knew quite what to do with him. Anna Pike and Wayne Noseworthy were eventually released from hospital, one with chronic asthma from a punctured lung, the other in a wheelchair with a useless leg and a stump. The other two also returned to class after Christmas; Jason White with a misshapen wrist which had been impossible to reset accurately, and Elizabeth Butler with ugly scars on her face. They were all assigned space in the Grade One classroom, with an assistant to help the disabled, and general supervision from the Principal. The whole school watched over them with special care, and asked solicitously after their injuries.

Philip, of course, had no scars to be asked about. His older sister Jane, who was in Grade Four, had friends whose brothers or sisters had been killed or maimed in the tragedy, and she poured her sympathy over them all, as did everyone else. Charlene Winsor, in particular, was greatly pitied as she had lost twin sisters, and all the girls clamoured to sit next to her and offered to share their lunches and walk home with her after school. No-one was interested in Jane. She came home one day very upset, because her best friend Elaine had been assigned to sit next to Charlene, and when Jane had objected, she was told she should be ashamed of herself for not caring about Charlene and was given the cold shoulder all afternoon. Her mother wasn't really listening to her story, so she turned on Philip and shouted that the least he could have done was get shot in the arm, so she had something to cry about. She realized as soon as the words were out of her mouth what a terrible thing she had said and smothered him with hugs and kisses, but he never forgot the look on her face when she said the awful words, and he knew he had let her down.

Philip hadn't let his mother down. She had dubbed him a saint and a miracle for avoiding the fate of his classmates, and he resolved with all his strength to play this role for her. His father had been lost on a bird hunting trip two years before, and his mother and sister were all he had in the world to cling to. His mother had told the reporters he had been very brave, never shed a tear or made a fuss, so that is what he continued to do, even though, after the numbness had faded, he had a pain inside his chest that grew harder and tighter every day until he could hardly breathe. Sometimes at night, when everything was really quiet, he would allow the hot salt tears to run down his face, clamping the blanket firmly between his teeth to keep back the sobs. Then the pain would go away for a while, and he could sleep. He came to realize that the pain got worse when the image of the gunman and the flashes and the cries and the blood were strongest, so he began to build a wall in his mind, block by block, to keep them out. It was very hard at first, but slowly the wall got higher until he could only glimpse shadows thrown against the roof, and then nothing but the rafters, and finally the wall was there all the time, and his memories of the incident were detached and impersonal, like a story in a book.

* * *

The Harrison Memorial Stadium had been closed since the tragedy, but by the next Fall there were murmurs about reopening it or building a new arena. Ice hockey was a strong tradition in the town, which had boasted a provincial Herder Cup trophy in its heyday, when Eddie Harrison played the front line. The town council thought about ripping the inside out and refurbishing it completely, but others thought they should build from scratch, and in a different location. The trouble with that idea was not only the great expense, but that the Harrison family had donated the land as well as the means to build the original stadium. It was tricky to weigh the sensibilities of a town patron against those of the victims' families. Mildred Harrison was in favour of renovating and incorporating a plaque to the victims. Others thought this crass and insensitive. One councillor, who would later represent the province in Ottawa, showed his political acumen by suggesting the present stadium be demolished and a park of remembrance be established on the site, commemorating both Harrison and the victims; meanwhile, application could be made to the Philip Greene Fund for the wherewithal to build a new arena.

This idea was debated with great interest until word of it reached Mrs. Greene. She was incensed that they would even consider using "her Philip's money" for such a thing. She had visions of scholarship funds in the future, as Philip was a bright little boy, and certainly none of the surviving children had any interest in skating or hockey. A bitter battle was fought in the corner stores, the Legion Hall, the church basements, and even in the schoolyard. It had one very important outcome as far as Philip was concerned. The straggled remnants of the Kindergarten class were drawn together in self defence, and he found a friend and ally in Anna Pike, whom he had worshipped in silence since they joined school together.

The question of the arena was settled on neutral ground, when the neighbouring town of Maiden Cove raised funds with the help of local businesses and a wealthy, nostalgic ex-patriot to build their own stadium, which then served the whole area. Harrison Memorial faded and peeled, its windows broken and boarded, its car park invaded by dandelions and blood-red sorrel. Several years later, it was quietly demolished, following the death of Mrs. Harrison, and a new town hall was built on the site, with a tastefully small brass plaque in the council chamber, recording the dreadful deed.

* * *

Elizabeth Butler had received gun shot wounds to her face, shattering her cheek bone, and deep cuts from her partner's ice skates, as they fell together. Her face had healed lopsided, with a deep gouge across one side, and two years later it seemed to be getting worse, causing dental and sinus problems. The local specialist was reluctant to tackle the task of reconstruction himself, but he recommended a plastic surgeon in the States, who was having great success with a new bone growth and laser treatment. Unfortunately, this procedure was outside provincial health care coverage. Elizabeth's family turned to the Philip Greene Fund.

When Wayne Noseworthy's mother heard about this from her sister-in-law's aunt, who worked in the same hospital, she started making enquiries about further assistance for Wayne. The doctors had promised he would be fitted with a prosthesis for his amputated leg, but there had seemed little point when the other leg was numb and incapable of bearing his weight, so he was still chairbound. The sister-in-law's aunt managed to get an appointment for Wayne with a visiting neurosurgeon, and the possibility of treatment for the paralysed leg was mentioned. Yet another specialist in the States was receiving attention in the medical journals for a new approach to spinal paralysis, but it required six months to a year of regular therapy, based in Houston, Texas. Again, the provincial health plan could not justify this expense.

The two major applications were filed with the trustees of the Philip Greene Fund within a couple of weeks, and it put them in a bit of a quandary. If both projects were fully approved, then the fund would be virtually wiped out. They decided to defer ruling on the applications until all interested parties had been consulted. Family representatives of all five surviving children were summoned to the bank boardroom. It might have been wiser to interview them one at a time, but instead, the trustees exposed themselves to the full primeval force of motherhood defending its young from would-be predators. The meeting began in a civilized fashion, with everyone agreeing that everything possible should be done to help Elizabeth and Wayne, but once it became clear how this would deplete the fund, the sympathetic murmurings turned to indignation and anger. Why should only two of the children benefit from all the money? They had all undergone the same ordeal. Why, if it wasn't for the saintly behaviour of Mrs. Greene's Philip and the miracle of his survival, there probably wouldn't be a fund. So how could they deprive him of it? He was a bright boy, he would go far, and he deserved the head start that the fund would give him. Neither righteous rage nor tearful pleading could penetrate Mrs. Greene's firm conviction that a good part of the fund belonged to Philip.

With the wisdom of Solomon, the trustees decreed that the fund should be divided into five equal shares, to be held in trust for each child until the age of eighteen, unless good cause could be shown for releasing it to the family before then. Philip's scholarship was secured, but the Butlers and the Noseworthys were forced to settle for second best treatment, or appeal to the local community to make up the difference. It says much for the deep-seated generosity and charitable nature of Newfoundlanders that they managed to raise enough money to send both children to the States, though Elizabeth had to cope without the company and support of all her family, and Wayne's father had to find temporary work in Houston to finance their extended stay, while his wife held the fort at home. The other three families were treated like lepers.

* * *

There was a general sigh of relief from the teachers, and from the community as a whole, when the "rump", as they were secretly called, eventually graduated from Grade Six and moved to the integrated high school in Maiden Cove. A replacement teacher was finally hired, and the recreational room turned back into a regular classroom with a full enrollment. A new generation, which had no direct memories of the tragedy and could treat it as a page in the history book, filled the school. Philip had also achieved that same stage in his private wall by now, and it was about this time that the stadium was demolished. The town could turn its back on the troubled past and begin to build its future.

* * *

Jason White had always lagged behind the others at school. His weak wrist made writing difficult, and he couldn't play most sports as his grip was poor. The rump as a whole were shunned by the "normal" classes, and within the group he didn't fit either. He and his older brother had been raised reluctantly by aging grandparents, after their mother ran off to Alberta with a neighbour, and their father spent long hours in St. John's, working occasionally and drinking constantly. Jason's defiant rudeness, and even petty thievery, were tolerated by the teachers in Trunkie Bay, who sympathised with his circumstances and did what they could to assist the grandparents. The Principal helped them apply to the trust fund for Jason's share of the money, as they were not well off, and Jason's father rarely contributed to the kitty. However, this weakness of character was obviously inherited, for the grandfather regularly advanced his son loans from Jason's money to fund ventures that failed, or trips in search of jobs that he couldn't even keep long enough to earn his stamps.

By the time Jason was thirteen, his share of the fund was exhausted, his grandmother dead, and all attempts at controlling him or his brother abandoned. Within the year, they were both in the reform school at Whitbourne, following charges of drug-dealing, malicious damage, theft, and assault. Jason's future was assured.

Philip's mother, reading about the court case in the paper, congratulated herself on how well she had managed to raise her son. Jason's lawyer had made much of the tragedy of his early life to try and mitigate the sentence, and the judge had acknowledged it. But her Philip had gone through the same ordeal, and was a good, quiet, hard-working boy, much praised by his teachers, and a credit to them all. It was nonsense to suggest that such an experience was bound to lead to trouble.

* * *

In high school, Philip and Anna Pike were the only two of the rump left. Wayne and his father had moved permanently to Texas, still hoping the therapy would work. Elizabeth, whose face was quite improved, dropped out of school at sixteen to train as a hairdresser and beautician. Her passion in life was to overcome ugliness, and she was fast becoming a master of disguise and counterfeit in her chosen profession.

Anna's health was delicate, and her regular asthma attacks meant that she missed a lot of school time. Philip made sure that she kept up with the work, spending long hours on evenings and weekends going over proofs and helping with essays, review questions, and projects, which they always did jointly. This was a labour of love on his part, for he had never outgrown his crush on her, and she repaid him with a fierce loyalty and friendship. He had no other friends in school, a fact overlooked by his teachers, who never missed an opportunity to praise his work and good conduct in class as a role model for the rest The resentment that had built up against him in Trunkie Bay, through no small effort of these teachers and his mother, followed him to Maiden Cove by the normal uncharted routes of schoolyard, playing field, park, and clubhouse. The only pleasure in his life was caring for Anna and working hard to please his mother.

Anna, despite her frailty, was a very attractive girl. She had fine red-gold hair, that curled silkily around her elfin face with its tiny turned-up nose, and milky skin that barely concealed the delicate blue veins of her neck and wrists. Her deep green eyes were fringed with golden lashes, which she lowered whenever a smile flickered over her finely curved lips. Irish myths, telling of the fairy princess who held sway over young men's hearts, were realized in Anna. And Philip was certainly not the only young man to appreciate such charms. Anna had refused, rebuffed, and ignored countless propositions, both serious and frivolous, polite and lewd, during her school years, but she saved her sweetest smiles for Philip.

Rod Powers was particularly bitter about being spurned by Anna. He was a couple of years older, and had lost his little sister in the massacre. He had never come to terms with why Anna and Philip had survived and she hadn't, and he resented the money that was poured on them. His gang of buddies had never lost an opportunity to make life miserable for the survivors, whenever adult eyes were averted, and it was Rod who prompted the smear campaign that had Anna's name vilified in every public washroom around the bay.

On Twelfth Night, old Christmas Day, 1986, Philip was walking Anna home after dinner. It was a clear moonlit night, and icicles, growing on the ends of branches after the sleet storm of the New Year, glittered like witches' talons. They took a short cut behind the town hall and across the swimming hole, which was now frozen solid. As they approached the trees on the far side, a group of lads dressed in old skirts, shawls, and rubber boots, and masked with pillow slips daubed with paint and holes cut for eyes and nose, rushed out at them. It was a little late for Christmas mummering, but this old tradition had recently found a new lease of life, and was a great excuse for the local rowdies to have a fling, now they had outgrown Hallowe'en.

"Hey, mummers, fine mummers here!"

"Give us a whirl, Anna, my little ice maiden!"

"Can't say no to the mummers, girl."

"Oh look, it's Miracle Boy! Walking on water, eh, Miracle Boy?"

The gang jostled round them, grabbing Anna by her arms and scarf and tugging her across the ice, calling her all the names off the washroom walls.

"Slut!" "Bitch!" "Dyke!"

"Hey, little Saint Philip, have you done her yet? Is she any good?"

"Let's show him how, boys!"

Philip stood rooted to the spot, a familiar numbness creeping through his body. The mummers had Anna down on the ice now, and were tearing at her clothes. One of the gang lurched across Philip and fell on the rum bottle that slipped from his pocket and smashed. The fellow cursed and shook his hand, splashing blood darkly over the ice. Anna was moaning as the biggest lout flung himself on her, fumbling with his belt, and released all his drunken anger, lust, and triumph. Two others followed him. The wall that Philip had built, block by block, to shut out the obscenity he couldn't deal with, the violence he had witnessed and been unable to stop, came tumbling down. He saw the bodies struggling on the blood-stained ice, smelt the fear and hatred, heard the cries of prey and predators. The bile rose hot and bitter in his throat, and he bent over and vomited. When he finally raised his head, the mummers had vanished into faint echoes of coarse laughter, and Anna lay shivering, her thin chest heaving for every rasping breath, and her pale legs gleaming in the cold green light of the winter moon.

It was Anna's father who found them. Anna was comatose by then, and was rushed to hospital, barely clinging to life. Philip was taken into custody, dazed and stinking of rum and vomit, the prime suspect. Anna's father had hurled abuse at him and almost throttled him before others came running. Asked to account for himself, Philip would say nothing, but just stared blankly ahead. He was remanded in custody, and even his mother could not argue for his release until after the lab results came in, which showed others were to blame.

But Philip knew where the guilt lay. He had always known, he realized now. He was the one who had been spared in order to save the others from the gunman, and he had failed. He hadn't moved a muscle in their defence. And he had just failed again. He had allowed Anna, whom he thought he loved more dearly than life itself, to undergo a fate worse than death, and he had not even uttered a cry. His mother and his teachers were wrong. He was a worthless bit of shit, just as Rod Powers had always told him, and he didn't deserve to live.

Philip's father had owned two guns, and after he drowned, they were packed away in the basement. His mother couldn't bear to part with them or even to think about them. Philip had first discovered them a few years ago, but left them alone, knowing how his mother felt. The day after he was set free, he waited until his mother had gone to work and then went in search of them. He chose the shot gun and carefully loaded the two cartridges still left in his father's ammunition belt. He took off his shoes and socks, held the gun balanced on its butt, pointing at his head, and manoeuvred his toe over the trigger. The first barrel failed to discharge, but on the second attempt he shot off half his face.

* * *

The event went unnoticed except in the shoreline weekly paper, and there was a brief twenty second report on the local CTV newscast. If any other reporter scratched his head and wondered why the name was vaguely familiar, he didn't bother pursuing it. The global village had its eyes raised to a clear blue sky over Florida that day, watching erratic plumes of white smoke from a fireball called Challenger spiralling down towards the Atlantic ocean. A class of excited children watched their teacher explode into history, and in no time at all they were surrounded with counsellors and psychologists to ease their trauma and comfort them through the horror of their experience. Perhaps Philip Greene would have been happy to know that.

The End

Scalping the Lord

November mists rolled gently over the Limagne Plain stretching eastward from the gates of the cathedral city of Clermont. Dawn cast its pale illumination on the Auvergne hills, which gathered protectively around the ancient town, and a platform with an elaborate throne was revealed, raised a little distance from the gates. Soon there would be clusters of clerics, restless knights, and curious townsfolk, drifting like fallen leaves winnowed by the prevailing wind, gathering around the platform to await the Word of God.

The Word was still evolving in the mind of God's Vicar, and he had spent half the night on his knees, seeking the final inspiration for his momentous appeal. Tall and noble of countenance, his fine beard streaked with the labour and stress of his fifty-three years, he stood now by the window of the bishop's apartments, watching the rising sun, and knew that he held the keys in his hands.

Even from his childhood, Odo de Lagery had shunned the traditional military career of a younger son of French nobility, and instead concentrated his fine intellect on the niceties of canon law and the ecclesiastical hierarchy. He had found rapid advancement in the clerical ranks and had become a favoured protégé of Pope Gregory. The route to the ultimate reward, the papal throne, was not so easily won, however, and Odo had borne full witness to the power of the sword in thwarting the ideals of the Church. He embraced peace whole-heartedly himself, but not in the lily-livered manner of his predecessor, Pope Victor III. His own shrewd and persuasive diplomacy had finally won him freedom from the clutches of the German Emperor, election to the papacy, and the upper hand against his rival anti-pope. He had bought his way into Rome rather than fight its citizens. He had made an ally and spiritual vassal of the rebellious son of the Emperor.

But he had known his limitations, and stopped short of demanding political concessions from the other princes of western Christendom. Instead, by steady exertion of canon law against the corruption of lay interference in the appointments and business of the Church, he had won respect as the spiritual leader of Europe. But all around him was evidence of the destructive powers of armed ambition, and from the east came regular reports of the violation of shrines and churches, pilgrims, and Christian states, at the hands of the heathen Infidels. The Eastern Emperor himself had been seeking his support.

The vision, sparked originally by the fervour of his patron, Gregory, had been growing in him for some time, but over this last summer he had been refining it, blending all the elements, and testing the reactions of his colleagues as he travelled around his native land. It was to be revealed today in his clarion call to arms for the Peace of God, Christian piety, and the achievement of that blessèd goal, on Earth as in Heaven, the Holy City of Jerusalem.

Visionary indeed was the promulgation of Crusade in this year of one thousand and ninety-five, directing all the aggressive, restless energy of the Frankish peoples against the enemy without, beyond the pale of Christendom. At stake was not only the recovery of the Holy Places, but the unity of the Christian Church, east and west, and the unequivocal position of the Bishop of Rome as prime mover, leader, and dispenser of rewards, temporal and spiritual. To bind to his command those proud and violent warriors, at whose hands he had suffered capture and humiliation, to have them kneel at his feet in humble repentance to receive their swords and symbolic cross: there was real power. And to achieve it he would never have lifted a sword himself against any man. He was a true follower of Jesus Christ, winning men with words and wonders, not threats and thunderbolts.

But these words must be carefully chosen. The special sanctity of Jerusalem, the goal of their military pilgrimage, was a focal point. The lands they conquered in the pursuit of this goal would be theirs for the taking (and what relief that would bring to the overcrowded fiefdoms of Europe), but it must be done in God's name and under His Leadership, with the full blessing and guidance of His Church.

Pope Gregory had seen himself at the head of a great army descending on Jerusalem, but Odo had no stomach for that. A papal legate would carry his authority by proxy. He already had his loyal candidate, good Bishop Adhemar of Le Puy, whom he had primed for this role just a couple of weeks before. On cue, he would fall at the Pope's feet and beg to be allowed to undertake the mission, and with luck, this emotional appeal would carry the crowd with him.

The urgency of the situation must also be stressed. Strike while the passion was hot, and before other ventures, closer to home, took their interest. The Church would guarantee the safe-keeping of their lands, wives, and chattels while they were away. And in case the direct appeal to their sense of pious outrage, and the underlying promise of material benefits, was not enough, he had another ingenious angle to play.

For the first time in the Church's history, he would offer all those who took up the Cross full remission of earthly penance for all their sins: a plenary indulgence. In one act of contrition and militant pilgrimage, a man could slough off the accumulated sins of his life without facing a plethora of fasts, flagellations, penalties, pilgrimages, and prayers. He would still have to answer to God after death, of course, but here too there was help available. The Church was always willing to intercede with the Lord (for a price), and offer prayers and masses for the souls of the dead. A most satisfactory arrangement all round. The Church could hardly lose.

Odo lifted his handsome head to the hills, now glowing rosily, and made his benediction. He turned to call his servant and priest to help him don his robes of office. Within the hour, the splendour of Rome would mount the platform in the person of Pope Urban II, and proclaim the greatest enterprise the Church had ever undertaken.

* * *

Fast forward three hundred years. Another pope, another call to arms. (Actually, make that two popes, two calls, as the King of France had his own pocket pope stashed away in Avignon.) But Boniface IX was not a man of the same stature, erudition, and intelligence as Urban II, and this crusade was a last ditch effort by emperors, kings, and princes to save the Eastern Empire from the Turks. Jerusalem had long since slipped from the hands of the earlier crusaders. But one thing Boniface did have was a good grasp of papal fiscal policy. The plenary indulgence, that fast-track ticket to Heaven, had proved most profitable, and all kinds of endeavours were now financed by their means. Jubilee years had been introduced (Boniface actually had two of them in ten years, why wait for the biblical fifty), which were bonanza times for the remission of sins. Crusading vows were regularly commuted, for a price. After all, Jerusalem was far more than just a pile of old masonry in a far off land, it was a spiritual temple, to be nurtured in the hearts of pious men.

* * *

. "A pitcher of ale for my friend here, good host! His throat must be parched as the sheepskin he sells, after that fine sermon."

The keeper of the Tabard Inn, on London's south bank, grinned and nodded at the portly gentleman addressing him. The fellow often visited his establishment and made dialogue with all manner of men to be found there. He loosened their tongues with a flagon of good cheer and timely compliments, and then he sat back and listened, a gleam in his eye and an encouraging smile always ready on his lips. No story was too coarse for him, no boast or brag protested as beyond belief. He took in everything that came his way, and by the end of the evening he glowed as warmly as his guests, drunk on words rather than wine.

The hapless guest this day was a lanky blonde-haired fellow, pop-eyed and voiced like an angel. They had just come from St. Barnabas church, where the young man had been preaching to the crowds.

"Ah, you should have heard him. First he sings like a lark, tugging open all the purse strings for the Offertory, and bringing tears to the eyes of the matrons. Then he opens up his scrip and flourishes the mighty waxen seals of popes and cardinals; he reads aloud the exhortations to put aside the sins of the flesh – avarice, greed, pride, and envy; he encourages his audience to dedicate themselves to building God's Church – in particular, the new nave of Westminster Abbey.

"But then he soars to new heights on the wings of his own eloquence. He lifts them from their seats and brings them tumbling to his feet to confess their sins and buy his pardons. He conjures their minds with –"

Unable to restrain himself any longer, the Pardoner wrested the conversation from his genial advocate and began piping his own virtues. How he knew the darker side of men! There was no escaping his arguments in church. If anyone showed reluctance to relieve himself of a heavy conscience, and its weight in silver, the Pardoner would claim that the power of his relics and papal indulgences could not be extended to those whose sins were too horrible to confess, or to a woman who had cuckolded her husband. They may as well just stay seated. Then, what a rush there was to prove one's virtue and piety, by buying the means to those very ends one had thereby exhibited! Socrates himself could not confound with stricter logic the simple minds of these poor sheep, clamouring to redeem their own shorn skins.

And what a wealth of choices he had in his possession for their salvation! Beyond the simple parchment pardon, he could offer holy relics and items blessed by saints and popes to work God's miracles. A knuckle of St. Peter to rap on Heaven's Door; a scrap of Holy Virgin's veil, stained with tears, to heal all wounds; splinters of the Holy Cross, some blushed with blood; hair from the severed Baptist's head; an arrowhead of Saint Sebastian's martyrdom; straw from the Christ Child's manger crib: an endless catalogue of marvels.

Refreshed by his ale and the interest of the landlord's other patrons, the Pardoner found his golden tongue once more. Somehow he contrived, between mocking the country yokel and aping the over-pious grande dame, to make his listeners feel they were astute enough to know a good deal when they found one. And then out came the rag and bone bag, each tiny scrap encased in a sealed casket and held on high to cries of wonder and amazement. Save the lack of cross and altar cloth, it was St. Barnabas all over again.

"I thank you, Master Chaucer, for your good patronage." The innkeeper leaned towards his friend with eyes a-twinkle. "This one's worth a crowd of curious bargain-hunters, who'll be thirsting after more than their salvation by day's end. You could write a merry tale or two, I do believe, of all the men whose stories you have listened to in here."

"I may just do that one day, my friend. I have a mind to share our fun with others."

* * *

"Pietro, what are we going to do with them? Look, the queue is so long now, you can't see the end." And Michele leaned out from his vantage point in the little turret room above the box office, craning his neck to follow the line as it dwindled down the hill.

"It is not for us to decide, Michele. Those first ones, in the white strip with the red crosses, that was not such a problem. Il Signore looked over the tickets himself. He was quite impressed with the workmanship, even if they did lack the special code. He let most of them in. He's very fair that way. He likes to give credit for ingenuity. But He made a careful note of the touter. He'll call in the favour when he's ready."

"But this latest bunch, they haven't even bothered to get the right card stock. And see how the printing's all blurred and faded? Mass production. No pride in craftsmanship these days."

"I'll take them up to Il Figlio's suite. He had serious doubts about that last lot. He didn't think His Father would want it to get out of hand. You let one in because you admire their cheek, and before you know it, everyone's in on the act."

"Well, He'll have to do something soon. There's such a crowd now, that the genuine ticket holders won't be able to get near the gates. The meek may inherit the earth, but they don't stand a chance of getting into this heavenly game without a bit of help from the heavies."

The phone rang, and Pietro stood to attention while he answered it. "Yes, Signore . . . You are quite right as always, Signore. We will see to it straight away." He put down the receiver and turned triumphantly to his fellow gate-keeper. "Well, Michele, the Word has come down! Tell Giorgio to get the enforcers out there and break up the mob. No more admissions except on Il Figlio's personal say-so. That should put an end to this particular scam for a while."

* * *

[Raising eyes slowly from contemplation as organ notes fade.]

"Oh, my sinning brethren! O Lord, have mercy on our souls, for we have gravely offended Thee. And you too, sisters, for are we not all equal in the sight of the Lord?"

[Wait for murmurs of assent.]

"We all have our sorrows, our regrets. The angry word we would have recalled. The comforting gesture we did not make. And some of us have far worse crimes on our conscience. Oh yes, far worse! Who among us has not wished harm to another of God's creation? Who among us has not nurtured a grudge against one closest to you – a mother or a father, a wife or a brother?"

[Pan congregation, look for guilty faces.]

"Who has not had covetous thoughts about his neighbour, or his neighbour's wife? A young girl in the street? The grocery boxboy? Vile unclean fantasies!"

[Loud and threatening.]

"Be honest with yourselves, brothers and sisters! Do not hide from your sins! Who among ye can deny these charges?"

[Quiet and repentant.]

"I cannot deny them. I stand before you as tarred and tainted as any soul in the whole of this congregation. I have sinned, oh grievously have I sinned! I have borne grudges. I have nourished hatred in my heart. I have had salacious dreams. I have given way to the weakness of the flesh."

[Close up, full unflinching eye contact.]

"Oh yes, I do not deny the scurrilous scandals of the supermarket press, though they hound me day and night. Their taunts and barbs will not hurt me. Their slings and arrows will not outrage me.

They cannot bring me to my knees. And do you know why?"

[Dramatic pause. Pan congregation for bewildered expectancy.]

"Do you know why, my sisters and my brothers? I think you do!"

[Pounding with fist.]

"The Lord has brought me to my knees! Oh yes, my friends, the Good Lord Jesus, Saviour of our Souls, Divine Pardoner, Salvation of the Sinner, the Lord our God has already brought me to my knees! He has come to me in the depths of my wickedness, in the hour of my despair, yea, in the very Jaws of Hell . . ."

[Hush.]

"And He has taken my hand, brothers and sisters, and led me into green pastures. And I have knelt at the true Fountain of Goodness and drunk of the pure waters of Forgiveness, Divine Forgiveness. You see me here today a changed man. A blessèd man. A man in the uniform of Christ, our only Saviour."

[Smooth sleeve of white linen suit, adjust red silk cravat.]

"I have taken up the Cross, my friends, the Cross of Jesus, and I will bear its weight on my shoulder for the rest of my life. For in return, I have received His Grace and Eternal Pardon for all my sins. So long as I carry His Cross, so long will He number me among the blessèd! But I need help, fellow sinners. I need help to carry this enormous burden for Our Lord."

[Look of earnest humility.]

"And you, brothers and sisters, you have the power! You have the strength! You can help me carry the Cross for Jesus, and you can walk with me in those green pastures of His Eternal Mercy. Together we can approach the gates of the Golden Jerusalem, the Heavenly City, and cast off our sins on the steps of Our Lord's Holy Vestibule, and enter His House clothed only in purity and light.

[Expansive smile.]

"Every dollar you send me, every pledge you make me, earns one small step, nay one giant leap, into that Holy Meadow! Come frolic with me, my friends, frolic in the heavenly fields of Divine Salvation! And may the Lord, and the taxman, bless your freely given generosity!"

[Hands together, pensive but serene. Roll screen with address and pledge numbers.]

The End

The Grey Havens

The snuff of old seasoned timbers, rain-battered daffodils, and fresh-turned earth would always stir this memory.

George stood beside his father in an English village churchyard and watched the vicar throw handfuls of dirt in his mother's face. For it was his mother who lay in the wooden chest with the polished brass hinges that had just been sunk into the cold wet clay. She was twice taken from him. The rigid, unresponsive mask on the silk pillow, that he had refused to kiss a few hours before, had already mocked his knowledge of her: full of life, angry and gentle, weeping and laughing by turn, a constant warm, solid presence through all his seven years. That frozen image, as false as the stiffly posed Sunday parlour portrait on the mantlepiece, would haunt the rest of his life. And now they were hiding her in the ground, stamping on her body, blotting her out, as the rain blotted his own pinched face.

George turned up his collar against the wind and freezing drizzle of a typical Newfoundland spring and abandoned his stroll along the rotting board walk in the park, where a stray dog was digging for bones in the beds of newly budding bulbs. He headed back towards the house that he shared with his daughter and her family in St. John's. He had a lot of planning to do, now that his doubts were resolved.

* * *

Ella was aware something was wrong. She had been sent to bed rather earlier than usual, following a phone call from her aunt which had put her mother on edge. There were other furtive phone calls after that, and she heard her parents talking long into the night. But that was all forgotten in the morning when she remembered that this was the day her Ganda was coming home!

Ella had grown up with her grandfather, who had lived with the family ever since his wife had died ten years before. He had been nursemaid, teacher, babysitter, storyteller, and mentor to her all her life and was as dearly loved as her parents. He spent time with his other daughter, too, but he and Ella had a very special relationship.

"Ella!" Her mother was a little too bright and brittle this morning. "Your Ganda probably won't be home today after all. It seems he's taking some time to visit old friends."

"But he said he'd be back today."

"I know, love, but he must have had a change of plan and forgotten to let us know. He has been a bit absent-minded lately. Aunt Stella says he left there a few days ago and was going to visit some old friends in Corner Brook."

"But why isn't he coming home today?"

"Well, if he's gone to Corner Brook it's a long drive. That's right over on the west side of the island. He'll probably call in at Aunt Stella's in Clarenville again on his way home and let us know when he's coming."

"But Ganda always keeps his word. He said he'd be here today!" Ella bit her lip to keep the tears at bay. He'd never let her down, and he'd promised they were going to finish rereading Tolkien's *Lord of the Rings* this week, their favourite story.

"Don't worry, love. I'm sure he'll be back soon."

But Marjory was worried. As Ella had said, it was most unlike her father not to tell them if he changed his plans, and she wasn't sure who he could be visiting in Corner Brook. No-one he had talked of lately. And he had changed recently; he was more withdrawn into himself, and he seemed suddenly to have got a lot older. Her sister, Stella, had noticed it too. She hadn't actually been sure he was going to Corner Brook, but when he talked about taking one last trip out west, she assumed that he was visiting friends there while he could still manage the long drive. He had lived in Corner Brook as a young man. Stella had been as nervous as Marjory when she realized he had not let her sister know his plans either.

They made discrete inquiries, but the police were not prepared to treat it as a missing person's case on such little evidence, and after so little time – only two or three days at most. Ella continued to look for his car every day when she came home from school, but she was always disappointed. She knew her parents were concerned, even though they made light of it, but she had every confidence that her Ganda wouldn't leave her without a word. He had told her that after JimJam's accident.

She had spent one glorious summer with her new puppy when she was five, but she had been careless. He had run out onto the street chasing her ball and was hit by a car. One minute he had been a bundle of energy and joy, and then he was whimpering in the gutter, his legs all mangled and his eyes slowly glazing over. She had wept hot salt tears over that quivering little body, blooded and soiled, which they later buried in the garden. She had nightmares for weeks, waking in a cold sweat with half-choked sobs. Her grandfather, in the next room, was always there to comfort her.

"Ganda, I dreamt you were JimJam and were lying in the gutter, all covered in blood, and it was my fault!"

"No, no, child, that wouldn't be me. You'll never see me like that," he told her. "And I'd never leave you without saying a proper goodbye, either. I'll always be your same old Ganda, larger than life and twice as foolish." He could always coax a smile from her. But he had meant what he said, she knew that. His eyes had burned quite fiercely when he said it.

* * *

A week after the day Ganda had failed to return, Stella called her sister with more disturbing news.

"Marjory, I was cleaning up Dad's room and looking for any clues as to where he might have gone, and I found his pills. His heart pills. They were tucked into a sock right at the back of the drawer. I'm sure they were deliberately hidden there. He normally keeps them on his bedside table when he's here. Do you suppose he's going dotty like Mother, hiding things away? Or what? Do you think he has any more pills with him? What if he gets the angina while he's driving? God, I'm getting so worried!"

Marjory decided to go and see the pharmacist and check if her father's prescription had been filled again recently. The date on the hidden bottle was a few weeks earlier. The pharmacist checked the computer and shook his head.

"I'm sorry, Mrs. Boland, there's no record of any later transaction. Maybe you should have a word with his doctor."

The next morning, the two daughters were sitting in Dr. Walsh's office. He peered at them over his reading glasses, looking up from the notes in the folder on his desk.

"Your father needs a supply of that medicine on hand day and night. He could get an attack at any time. He knows that, I made it very clear to him. But . . . there's another matter that I think you should know about, too. When he was in a few weeks ago, he was complaining about some abdominal pain and passing a bit of blood. He said he thought it was just haemorrhoids, but would I check it out. I understand his father died of bowel cancer, and I suspect he was really worried he had the same thing. Well, it wasn't haemorrhoids, and I told him I would set up some tests at the hospital and refer him to a specialist. He was supposed to go as soon as he got back to town last week. I gather he didn't tell you anything about this? I played it down a bit, but I think it could be serious, and the longer the delay, the worse the prognosis. If he is worrying about the tests, it could set off an angina attack."

They went immediately to the police after this and finally got a reluctant commitment to put out an alert for their father and his car. The police suggested they also try the radio stations. But the trail was rather cold by now, and no-one came forward with any sightings. The hospitals and the Port aux Basques ferry to Nova Scotia drew a blank, and no abandoned or wrecked cars bore the right licence plate. George Drake had disappeared.

Marjory and Stella were remembering their mother in her last years. She had died of pneumonia and complications resulting from Alzheimer's Disease, but it had started with occasional lapses of memory, hiding things which she then couldn't find, and wandering off and getting lost. Could their father be going the same way? It was much worse before the end. They had watched the mother they knew and loved forget who her daughters were, while fawning on strangers; get sly and underhand; shout at their father for no apparent reason and then cower as if he would hit her; laugh out loud in the middle of a friend's funeral service. Their father didn't take her out much after that, he was so mortified by the change in her. And then there was the incontinence.

"I don't know if I could go through all that again with another parent," said Marjory in despair. "It's like watching someone die in slow motion before your eyes, and you can do nothing about it." They gripped each other's hands, and sat silently for a while.

* * *

Ella came bursting into the kitchen one afternoon clutching a small package. She had seen the mailman on her way back from school, and he had given it to her.

"It's from Ganda!" she shouted. "It's his writing. Look!"

But the package was addressed to Miss Elanor Gamgee, 3021 Grey Havens, Vancouver, British Columbia, and had been returned to sender with a note that the address did not exist. The sender's name was Ella Boland. Marjory stared at her daughter in complete bafflement.

"What is all this? Who's this woman in Vancouver that you're writing to? What's going on?"

"It wasn't me, don't you see? It was Ganda. It's his writing."

And Marjory had to agree that it was. But what he thought he was doing, mailing letters to this unknown person and using his granddaughter's name as the sender, she had no idea. The ghost of her mother's illness shivered across her shoulders again.

"We had better open it then. Or maybe I should wait till your Dad's home. I'm a little worried about what we might find. Ganda hasn't been very well lately . . ."

The package had been mailed from Grand Falls, halfway between Clarenville and Corner Brook, about three weeks ago – two days before this whole fiasco started. Marjory called her husband and then the police, but meanwhile left the package untouched on the kitchen table.

Ella stared at the address, but then she had the first quivering of an idea. She hurried off to the bookcase in her room and took down the last volume of the *Lord of the Rings*. She started reading where they had left off, in the last chapter, where everyone in the Shire settles down to lead their normal lives again. She found the clues she was seeking. Sam Gamgee, Frodo the Ring-Bearer's faithful companion, had a daughter named Elanor. And September 29, 3021, by the Middle Earth calendar, was the date of the departure of the Ring-Bearers from the Grey Havens. It was suddenly all very clear to Ella what her Ganda was telling her.

"Mom, he's gone. Ganda's gone."

"I know, my love, but the police are looking for him. I'm sure they'll find him soon. We think he has probably just lost his memory, and sooner or later he'll turn up."

"No, he won't. He won't be found. He's left us and gone away, over the sea. Open the package and see." And Ella tried to explain to her mother about the Ring-Bearers and their burden, and how eventually they grow weary and sick of Middle Earth and sail off to the Uttermost West to find peace and happiness. Marjory was not a Tolkien addict and had never read the stories, but she felt her heart wrung by the innocence of her daughter's account. With tears in her eyes, she asked Ella what she thought was in the package.

"I don't know. Maybe a ring? Though the Elves took theirs with them. But then Ganda isn't exactly an elf, is he!" And she laughed lightly and happily at that image of her bald and paunchy Ganda!

Theirs was not a religious family, and Ella had not attended church or Sunday School, but she was as buoyed and confident in her sudden understanding of her Ganda's fate as any Christian believer. Marjory was disturbed by this, as perhaps any non-believer is. What did her daughter really think: that he had been spirited away somewhere, or taken up by an angel in a golden cloud? She surely couldn't take literally that Tolkien allegory, beautiful as it was. Marjory was haunted by images of an old sick man, confused and upset, wandering alone somewhere, or lying helpless with a broken hip. The possibilities were endless.

When Ella's father got home, accompanied by the police sergeant, they opened the package. And Ella beamed with delight at the proof of her theory. Inside lay a diamond studded ring in a little leather pouch and a note addressed to Ella. Marjory recognized the ring at once.

"It's my grandmother's engagement ring! My father used to carry it around with him always, until we persuaded him it wasn't safe. He must have been to the bank to get it from the safety deposit box. What was he thinking of, putting it in the mail to a fictitious address! How could he be sure it would come back? The package wasn't even insured! Why didn't he just give it to her? He said she was to have it after he was gone." And she broke down in tears that could no longer be resisted.

When all was calm again, Ella patiently explained to her father and the policeman what she had already told her mother, as they read the note together.

> "*The Grey Havens,*
> *Middle Earth.*
> *September 29, 3021*
>
> *My Dearest Ella,*
>
> *To the fairest Hobbit who ever lived, I entrust this ring, which I have carried long enough in this life. It was my mother's ring, and she did many good works with it in the short time spared to her, including producing your very own Ganda!*
>
> *I have tried to live a good life and to bring comfort and happiness to those who are dear to me, especially you. I don't want to be a burden to them or break my promise to you, that I would always be the same old happy-go-lucky Ganda. The time has come for me to go on my final voyage to the Uttermost West.*
>
> *Wish me joy and peace, my dear. And remember me as your ever loving*
>
> *Ganda*"

The police sergeant looked very solemn and signalled to Ella's parents that they should have a private talk. Ella took the ring, promising her mother to take good care of it, and wandered off to her bedroom, her head full of all the wonderful tales, games, treasure hunts, and puzzles her Ganda had concocted for her over the years. She was sad that they wouldn't be sharing them anymore, but he had not left her without saying a very special goodbye. She had known he would keep his promise.

"Well, sir, it looks very like a suicide note to me, strange as it is. You say you think he may have been getting a little confused lately? What did his doctor think?" The sergeant thought privately that the old man was obviously completely mad, but he had to be diplomatic.

"Ella and her grandfather used to play a lot of games. They'd act out the stories they read together, and he was always setting up little clues and puzzles for her to follow. We have the most popular birthday parties on the block, you know!" Ella's father was embarrassed by the note and trying to explain it away. But the sergeant was right. However crazy the context, the intent was clear. They would have to start looking for a body now, rather than a sick or senile wanderer. He turned to comfort his distraught wife, who had just called her sister with the news. The possibility that had been at the back of all their minds was now looming monstrously large.

"How could he have done this!" Marjory was red-faced with tears and anger. "Doesn't he realize how worried we are, were bound to be? We could have coped. We coped with Mother. Why did he have to hide it all? How are we ever going to make Ella understand after all these silly games? He's totally irresponsible!"

And the long, slow process of the daughters' grieving was begun, with no hope of an end to it as long as George Drake was somewhere out there, fate unknown.

* * *

George walked out of the post office in Grand Falls and congratulated himself that everything was going to plan. He reckoned it would take nearly a month for that package to get back to St. John's and put Ella's mind at rest. He felt badly about leaving her in the dark so long, but he had to give himself time to get well and truly lost. He patted his breast pocket, where he had hidden two of his pills for emergencies along the way, and then walked down to the Canadian Tire store.

Several hours later, he was driving down an old logging road in the upper reaches of the Humber River. Fortunately, the road was still hardened with frost at this time of year and its snow cover flattened by snowmobiles. A small four-wheel drive vehicle was one of the luxuries he allowed himself, and it coped well with the winter conditions. After a couple of hours of steady progress, he reached the turn-off he remembered from earlier years and started down it. The skidoos had not penetrated far this way, and soon he was finding it heavy going. He took one last run at a partial clearing by the track and drove the vehicle into the trees, where it eventually came to a halt buried in snow up to the axles. He got out the axe and cut some boughs to cover the vehicle.

He strapped on his snowshoes, shouldered the backpack, and then set off through the trees, pushing his way as best he could through the narrow gaps. He didn't make more than a mile or so before darkness and his own exhaustion forced him to stop and hollow out a shelter under a couple of large intertwining trees. He lined it with a plastic sheet and crawled into his sleeping bag. He nibbled at a couple of granola bars from his meagre supply, had a quick tot of rum, and fell into a weary but fitful sleep.

The weather warmed up a little overnight and brought a fresh fall of snow, over ten centimetres, which blanked out the tracks and completed the camouflage of his vehicle. It also formed an extra blanket over George and kept him warm enough to face another day.

Many years before, when his father had been dying in the Corner Brook hospital, hooked up to tubes and bags that fed and evacuated him, and hovering between a state of morphine-induced coma and horrendous pain, George had fled his visiting duties for one day and taken a day's fishing in this area. The tranquility of the woods, barely punctuated with bird song, and the steady swirling of the icy water over rocks into deep pools had calmed his mind, and he had thought how much more fitting a setting this was to take leave of life than the one his father was experiencing. And this had come back to him when he read in Dr. Walsh's face the grave omens of his own future. If death was invincible, he could at least make the ground rules and choose his weapon. He took the two emergency pills from his pocket and hurled them into the trees. He had got this far undetected, the snow was his cover, and he didn't need to further prolong the process.

George felt a slight guilt about deceiving his daughters. They wouldn't like this unconventional behaviour. They would rather have suffered the responsibilities of dutiful family care, an uneasy martyrdom bolstered by the sympathy and respect of friends, and the knowledge that it couldn't last forever. He knew it well; he had nursed his own wife through her unwitting ordeal. Many times he had wondered if he was really acting for the best. Occasionally she would have moments of clarity and self-knowledge, and he caught a look of despair and pleading in her eyes. Then he wanted to set her free, like a trapped rabbit, ending the misery with a quick blow. But he couldn't do it. Fear replaced despair so quickly, and it would have been like putting down a sick dog, cowering in its corner, that didn't understand how it had offended.

He had once seen a program about a nomadic people in central or southern Africa, pygmies or bushmen, he couldn't remember exactly, who had a custom which struck him at the time as both awful and enlightened. When the elderly members of the group became too sick or weak to keep up with the constant movement required to find new sources of food, they were abandoned. A special hut was built, and the old person was laid inside with a supply of food and water. Ceremonial farewells were made, paying respect to the person and his contribution to the society, and then the group moved away. The elder was left to die alone, his dignity intact. All trace of him, bar a few bones, would be gone by the time his people returned to those parts later in the annual cycle. Modern civilization would not accept such simplicity. Maybe Ella would share his vision through Tolkien's allegory. They had shared so many moments of wisdom between their laughter and tears.

The day passed slowly. George left his sleeping bag only to stretch his stiffening legs and to relieve himself. He thought about struggling on further through the trees to try and find his old watering hole, but the snow was light and deep, even for snowshoes, and he didn't know which way to head. Another night gave way to dawn, more snow fell, and George had finished his food rations and most of his rum. His feet were numb, his legs cramped, and excruciating pains were shooting through his abdomen. He was thirsty, but mouthfuls of snow offered little relief. He now felt too weak to drag himself clear of the sleeping bag, and when he could hold out no longer, he soiled his clothes. He had uncontrolled fits of shivering, and he spilled the last drop of rum while fumbling with the cap. His mind was wandering, but the pain in his bowels kept bringing him back to reality. He cursed his heart for not finishing him off long before this.

Later that afternoon, he heard the whine of a snowmobile in the distance and was tempted to cry out, but his voice was no more than a croak, and the machine passed by him a few hundred yards away on a path the other side of the thicket. His misery was compounded by the realization that he would have welcomed being rescued at this point, despite his lofty ideals. Darkness and the eery silence of the winter woods settled around him once more, and the temperature finally began to plummet. Trees creaked and protested the icing of their sap, already rising to the promise of spring, but George sank into a state of numbed torpor and was relieved at last, by his fickle heart, of all his agony.

* * *

It was October before the ravaged remains were found by hunters and their dogs out rabbiting, a few days after the abandoned vehicle was identified. A funeral service was held in St. John's, at which George's daughters wept with mingled feelings of loss and relief. They had buried their father and could now get on with their own lives. Ella, however, was just beginning a lifetime of doubt and disillusionment all too familiar to her grandfather.

The End

Author/Subject

Lifting her eyes from her scribbled notes, she drifted through the living room down the long, long street with her book clutched under her arm. The bearded face on the cover stared arrogantly from the crook of her elbow. The houses passed quickly, as if she was on a moving walkway like the one at the airport, though she felt her legs were dragging. The book weighed heavily on her arm and she let it go. The pages fluttered silently on the sidewalk, disturbed by no breeze that she could feel. She turned aside and found she was in the meadow by the sea.

* * *

He picked himself up and dusted off his sleeves. He didn't know this place, but he made a quick note of the setting and direction and then followed the woman down the street.

* * *

She picked the daisies, and tongue between her teeth for added concentration, carefully made a slit in the stem of each one with her thumbnail. She threaded the heads through and soon had a long chain to hang around her neck and over her hair. A child again, she danced around the maypole and spun herself in a dizzy whirl until she fell flat on the warm, matted turf that smelled of summer. As the trees and sky spun around her head, she thought she glimpsed a face. The eyes gleamed darkly from behind a tree, the features muffled in a black curly beard. She tried to focus on the tree, her head still swimming, and as she stumbled to her feet she lost her balance again.

* * *

When he next became aware of his surroundings, he was standing in a small shed in a farm yard. It smelled strongly of wet wool and stale milk, and huddled in the corner on a bed of soiled straw lay a young lamb. Outside in the yard, a little girl in a buttoned-up coat was approaching with a large whisky bottle filled with milk and topped with a black rubber teat. She was breathing out slowly and deliberately, trying to make the frosty clouds obey some pattern, but gave up with a laugh when she saw she had no control. She looked towards him and suddenly froze. She turned and ran back to the house.

* * *

She was hurrying up the street, glad to be nearly home out of this postmidnight blackness.

She had missed the earlier train because the London show had run late. No buses this late, and no taxis around. Only an occasional lamp was still lit, and she paused briefly under each pool of light to peer anxiously into the surrounding gloom. She had run half the way from the railway station right in the middle of the road for fear of hands grabbing her. Not a soul was about except – oh dear God! a man up ahead marching towards her. The scream wouldn't come, but then she heaved a sob of relief. Her father's voice was calling out to her, angry and upset, but no more than she deserved for being two hours beyond her curfew. As they approached more closely, his figure in its belted raincoat was reassuringly familiar, and she started to run towards him. One more pool of light lay between them, and as he stepped into it she saw his face. Except that it wasn't his face.

* * *

He could see over her shoulder that the room behind the green baize door was shabby, like its occupant. Papers lay in untidy piles on the floor, participants in an outsize game of checkers with dirty coffee mugs, stained library books, and an assortment of discarded sweaters and socks. The professor was sunk in the scuffed leather opulence of an over stuffed armchair and bent over double as she contemplated the next move. The young woman edged into the room and closed the door. The professor beckoned her to sit on the sofa by the window, which looked down onto the cloistered courtyard. She sat down, avoiding the end which was spewing bristly horsehair from a mortal wound to its innards.

The young woman began to read her essay on the influence of the gutter press on social attitudes, but soon they were floating down the river with the professor huddled on the cushions at one end of the punt, while he worked the pole steadily in and out of the rippling water. As the woman continued to explain the influence of gutters on social platitudes, the punt grew longer, and the professor faded into the river mist. Still the young woman's voice droned on, describing the influence of gutting on platypuses, with which the river was now teaming. A muted roar could be heard as they approached the next bend, and he realized too late, as they were swung by the current, that they were on top of the weir. She finally turned around to look at him, just as he toppled off the punt, still clinging to the pole lodged in a grating.

* * *

Tom held her hand tightly and breathed with her. "Control it, love, control!"

The monstrous vice that was clutching her abdomen threatened to overcome her, but she lay there, gasping and goggling like a fish out of water, till the next wave of relief washed over her. The rollercoaster got steeper and faster till her whole being was focused on pushing the pain down and out of her body. Two searing moments later, and the pain had never existed. They hugged each other, sweat and tears mingled, and turned expectantly to the whitecoated professionals at the foot of the bed. The baby was nowhere to be seen.

"Where is she? Where's my baby?"

They leaned over her, soothed her brow, stuck needles in her hand, pumped hard on her abdomen, slipped her pills and a bedpan, tucked her in, and told her nothing. The whiteness around her was dazzling, muffling, suffocating and completely silent. Years passed, and still no one brought her baby. She struggled to keep her mind from disintegrating into ice crystals floating in all directions. Her mouth could barely form the words, "Where is she? Where is my baby?"

At last she saw him walking down the corridor with a bundle in his arms. He had on a long green gown and a mask covering his nose and mouth. She stared at the bundle, and as he approached, he drew back the corner of the blanket to reveal a large china doll.

"I'm sorry, Little Mother, I'm really sorry. Your baby is dead. You can't have her. You really should have taken greater care of her."

The stranger removed his mask, allowing the curly black beard to spring free, and casually let the doll fall toward the black and white tiled floor.

* * *

He was becoming increasingly frustrated. The woman fascinated him, but every time he got within reach, she shied away and he blacked out. When he came round again, the surroundings had changed, and the woman had aged. She treated him as a bogey man one minute, ignored him the next, but always the barrier came down before he could touch her. He decided to play a more subtle game. He willed himself into a more distant future, following the thin ribbon of road from where he had started his quest.

The old lady sat in the chair with her chin nodding down on her sunken chest. A smile twitched her lip from time to time, and he saw the remembered moments of pleasure in her feeble mind's eye as though it was his own. He waited quietly beside her and absorbed the fluttering images, until her head lolled suddenly to one side, and she opened her eyes in startled confusion.

* * *

The party was boring. Her legs ached from standing around in unaccustomed high heels, and her face felt stretched from an excess of polite smiling. She was on her fifth animated conversation about the deplorable state of something or other, spiced with yet another anecdote of someone's wife's brother's neighbour's dilemma. She put her brain on automatic pilot and let her senses rove the room. Strangely, her husband was not there. She only came to these functions at his insistence as a rule. His colleagues were over there by the bar, no doubt talking shop, and with them was Gavin. That was odd, because Gavin was someone she had known years ago, before she met Tom.

Until Gavin, her sexuality had seemed a liability, curbing her childhood freedom and intruding on her every interaction with the world. Gavin had made her rejoice in this new dimension to life. He had not come on to her when they first met, but rather they had become joking coconspirators against their mutual boss, who had employed them for the summer as cheap student labour. She had made the first move in fact, and any apprehension she might have felt was dispelled by his easy acceptance. The affair had ended with no lingering regrets when they went their separate ways at the end of the summer.

As she moved towards him, she felt the excitement flow through her body, concentrating between her legs, tingling in her breasts. He placed his hand on her shoulder, and brushing her cheek with his beard, breathed into her ear. A moment's panic. He had never had a beard, and across the room his face had been close-shaven! But his touch, his smell, the deep dark eyes, were surely as she remembered them. His fingers were slipping down her spine, following the contours of her naked body, seeking the source of her urgency. She shuddered with the sudden burst of pleasure, and again, and then her eyes were staring into the darkness of the bedroom. Her husband breathed gently at her side, and cold air was already chilling her sweat-ridden body where the sheets were thrown back. She pulled them up quickly and lay guilty in the black night, unaware of the dark bearded figure who had slowly withdrawn his hand and was lying, still as ditchwater, on the floor beside the bed.

She rose late the next morning, long after Tom had left for work. She hugged Mondays to herself as her own special days, earned by working Saturdays and running herself ragged on Sundays to catch up on housework. She picked up the folder from her desk in the little room she had prepared as her den, and where she dabbled at writing in her spare time. She had a couple of hours before her lunch date with two other truant friends, time enough to revise chapter four. She made herself comfortable on the living room sofa.

She read through the badly typed rough draft, with its pencilled alterations written in, scratched out, and rewritten in the margins. She sharpened her pencil and hunted for the soft pink eraser in the drawer. The ideas floated in her head like soap bubbles, iridescent with multi-shades of meaning, but on paper, reduced to black and white, they were lacklustre and obtuse. The central figure around whom she was trying to weave her rainbow was elusive. She had drawn a fairly convincing portrait of his character at the outset, and she had her plot sketched out, but now she was losing the thread of the story. He appeared wooden and contrived in some of her scenes, while slipping in and out of others almost without her noticing. She couldn't pin him down. Maybe she should ditch him all together and use a different angle. She scrawled heavy dark lines through her sheets of paper and filed them away. Maybe tomorrow she would feel more inspired.

She called her friends to confirm her lunch date. As she put down the receiver she thought she heard the door close, but no one was there when she looked.

"I'm getting so spooked lately," she chided herself. "First all these weird dreams, and now I'm hearing ghosts. I'll have to tell the girls – they'll probably say it's menopause setting in early!"

* * *

They all made a good lunch of her autobiographical dreaming (though she omitted to tell them the final details of the previous night). It was when she was looking for the waitress to bring them more coffee, to offset the two bottles of wine they had consumed, that she noticed him sitting in a booth at the back.

"You won't believe this," she mouthed at the others in a dramatic stage whisper, "but my bogey man is actually watching us right now!" And she rolled her eyes in his direction.

"What, the one over there with the beard? What fun!"

"Are you going to introduce us?"

And they all giggled like born-again schoolgirls.

She was not so amused when, driving home later a little bit tipsy, she noticed a large blue van following her. As she turned off the main road into her own piece of suburbia, it was still on her tail. In her rearview mirror she could see the dark curly beard. The back of her neck prickled under his gaze. She drove straight past her own house, back out on to the highway, and into town.

Tom was quite surprised to see her walk through the office door, and mildly curious about her sudden enthusiasm to eat out and do a show that evening straight from work, but his mind was on more important matters, and he didn't really listen to her improvised excuses. The movie relaxed her. Woody Allen's pathetic character and the ridiculous problems he faced, like a modern Chaplin, reaffirmed the normality of her own life. She was humming the title tune to herself in the foyer, waiting for Tom to bring the car round, when someone brushed by her, pulling up his coat collar. She saw the wisps of curly beard, and then he turned and nodded to her before swinging through the doors and out into the crowds on the street.

She kept Tom awake as long as she could that night, talking, teasing, and making love, but his mind was always half on the clock, and he had to rise early in the morning. She lay with her fists clenched, dreading more dreams, knowing he would be there. She didn't know what she was afraid of. He had never actually hurt her or threatened her, but the potential was always looming for an unpredictable turn of events and loss of control, of the past as well as the future, the unknown. It was like stepping off a cliff into thin air, but without the faith to fly.

She was wrong. She tossed and turned all night, in and out of dreams and nightmares, falling awake with a sudden thumping of her heart, and drifting off again. But nowhere did she see a dark bearded man, though she hunted through every surreal situation.

* * *

The dreams gradually subsided over the next couple of months, and she even forgot for days at a time to look out for the man in her everyday life. She seemed to have laid the ghost to rest.

She went back to her story several times, odd moments snatched at weekends and in the evenings, but she made little progress. Without her main character to pull the story together, the novel consisted of a series of vignettes, strung together like beads of dew on a spider's strand. Unlike the spider, she was unable to spin the strands into a coherent web, which would catch the reader's attention and keep him enthralled. Once again, she pushed the novel to one side and concentrated instead on crafting the dew drops into poetic pearls, to submit to the local literary magazines.

* * *

A few weeks after Christmas, Tom came home really excited. The firm had received a letter from an American client, who was interested in setting up a subsidiary office in Montreal and staffing it from London. Tom was to be the front man in the negotiations, and he had his ticket to leave tomorrow. The evening was taken up with her getting Tom's things together, while he studied a sheaf of reports and statistics.

"I have a real shot at this one, you know. If I make the right impression I could get the appointment as managing director over there. How do you fancy living in Canada, love?"

It was a rhetorical question, and the message was clear enough. If the job was offered he'd take it. She hardly had time to assimilate this possibility before he was gone in a flurry of briefcase, suithanger, tickets, and credit cards. But alone in the house the next few evenings, she gave it a lot of thought. New surroundings and friends, a new way of life, a new start. The unknown. She found it very uncomfortable.

* * *

Two days after Tom had left she saw the man again. He was at a checkout counter four down from her in the supermarket. Then he was leaving the dentist's office as she walked in, brushing by her without a look or a word. He was selling newspapers on the street as she left work the next afternoon. She locked and bolted the doors when she got home at night, calling out loudly before entering any room, leaving the lights blazing. She even checked under the bed, half grinning at her own foolishness, before jumping in. When the phone rang at two in the morning she nearly hit the ceiling.

"Great news, love! Oh sorry, did I get you out of bed? I was forgetting the time difference. I've got the job! You can come over and join me for a week, look for a house and so on. Then we can arrange the sale and all the other details in England from here. Let me know what plane you're arriving on. And charge the ticket to the company. Bernie will do all that for you. Must dash! See you soon."

She was not going. Her life as it was now was well under control. She had good friends of many years' standing, a secure job, and the little cottage down in Kent was almost paid for. When Tom took early retirement, they meant to live there most of the year. She would do her writing, he would tend the garden, and they would do things together. She had it all planned, and now he was striking out in a new direction without any apology or concession to her way of thinking.

Next morning, Bernie rang her at work to tell her he had her ticket waiting, if she would like to drop by the office. She started to tell him that she wouldn't need it, when the man with the beard walked into the reception hall, peering around him as if looking for something, someone. There was an air of purpose and menace about him, lacking before. She panicked.

"I'll be there in twenty minutes, Bernie."

She left by the staff entrance at the back of the building. When she picked up the ticket, she found she was to fly out that afternoon. The whole thing was preposterous. Her life was being cranked up like a Victorian phonograph in the hands of Frankenstein's monster, and the speed of events was making her dizzy.

* * *

She was not sure how she got there, but she was gliding along the moving walkway at Heathrow Airport, her ticket and passport in one hand, overnight bag in the other. Every time she had tried to get off the escalator, her path was barred by the man with the beard. He had grown taller, broader shouldered, more glittering of eye, more insolent in his stance. The white teeth glistening in the bed of black curls reminded her of a border collie, confidently and relentlessly herding his quarry towards the open gate. Now she stared at the skylines and landmarks of the world's cities as they flowed by her in a continuous line along the wall, like some long, neverending street. Obediently, she followed the arrows, stowed her luggage, and took her seat.

She sat in a trance, drinking and eating when the tray was put in front of her, not even looking out the window at the perfect sunny day above the clouds. Suddenly there was a hustle of activity, a crowd of people were leaning over her, some with cameras, all staring out of the plane.

"Below you on the right hand side, as we drop to thirty thousand feet, you will see the North Atlantic off the coast of Labrador and Newfoundland. This area is known as Iceberg Alley and has always been treacherous for navigation. Every speck you see will be an individual berg, some probably weighing in excess of two hundred thousand tons . . ."

The captain's voice droned on, explaining the phenomenon below, and she finally turned to look. The noise of the plane was suddenly muffled, but in her head she heard him saying, loud and clear,

"I'm sorry, Little Martha, I'm really sorry. Your life is over. You can't have it anymore. You really should have taken more control of it."

She fell from the plane, spiralling down in a torrent of soundless air towards the sea below. The sea was a coagulum of white ice and black shadow, but when she reached it she found it soft and dry. The whiteness was pulpy and fibrous, quite dry, and the dark shadows were in fact solid black blocks, cut in all kinds of intricate curves and angles. As she lay there, flat between the rows of blocks, she looked up at the paling sky which seemed to be closing down on her. The atmosphere was oppressive. She laboured with the stifling air and then gave up the struggle, sinking into blank oblivion.

* * *

He closed her book firmly, and tucking it under his arm, strode through the living room and out on to the long, long street.

The End

Flip

"That was fun," said Conjura. "Toss again." Imaginus flipped the coin, and it kept on and on spinning tales.

* * *

> (These characters were not really sure how they got here, but I think, as the author of their actions, that it had something to do with me taking a peek at the end of the story before I had fairly begun it.

> (This is an incurable habit of mine, which poses serious problems when reading a who-dunnit. The secret is to skim the final page down to the very last sentence, which is all I allow myself to read. I have usually decided who the likely culprit is by this time and am seeking confirmation, so that I can finish the story with a certain self-satisfaction. Contrast this with the action of someone I know, who will walk out of a movie with a couple of minutes left

to run, or stop reading a book in the middle, thinking they know what will happen. This story is for all of you like-minded cheats. You have just read the end, so now you can sit back and enjoy the path leading up to it, without any suspense or pre-conceived ideas.

(I have started with the end, so now I'll plunge into the middle, with total disregard for the rules.)

* * *

Peacock strutted slowly along the terrace beneath the stately French windows, keeping a watchful eye on his harem. A slight twitch of something bushy and red behind the wall caught his attention, and then came a softly teasing voice.

"Ah, what a wonderful tail Turkey has, quite the most splendid I have seen."

Peacock stopped and glanced all around. He couldn't see Turkey anywhere (which was not surprising, as he was bundled tightly inside Fox's big sack). He shrugged and resumed his inspection of the terrace.

"Dear me yes, that Peacock must be quite jealous, poor thing."

Peacock turned and glared at the sharp twinkling eyes peering over the wall, his vanity aroused. Slowly he raised his own tail and spread its canopy of iridescent colours aloft like a Caribana costume, swaying this way and that to catch the sun.

("What is . . . caribana?"

"You know, the big parade in Toronto, celebrating Caribbean culture."

"How weird! Never heard of it.")

"Dare to say that to my face, you wretched animal!" Peacock screeched. "Nothing can surpass this magnificence."

But quick as a flash, Fox jumped over the wall and grabbed Peacock by the neck before he could even think of closing his tail and flying off. Fox stuffed Peacock into the sack on top of Turkey, Grouse and Wren, who had all fallen for similar insults to their nether parts. Fox had a big family to feed, and he set off home with a big grin on his face, ready to tell his tale.

("That's not an original story, it's just a rehash of Chicken-Licken!"

"Exactly, it's a folk *tale*! I haven't finished yet, and by the way, that's a score of six for me so far.")

High in the sky, a red kite was drifting lazily, circling over the scrubland. Every so often it dipped down close to the ground then floated gently up again. A raucous flock of crows suddenly appeared, flapping and wheeling all around the kite, trying to scare it off. One of them caught the kite by its tail and tugged, ripping it off, and the kite plummeted towards the ground below. As fickle fate would have it, Fox was trotting along through the shrubs, congratulating himself on his cunning tricks, when the kite fell from the sky onto his head and broke his neck.

("OK, I'll give you another point for the kite's tail, but I claim a bonus one for the fox's head!")

* * *

The easternmost point of North America. It should have been thrilling, looking out across the ocean with nothing between herself and Ireland, but that was the trouble. There was nothing out there, just a thick bank of fog, mournfully acknowledged by the Cape Spear fog horn. She could barely see the jagged slabs of pink rock tumbling down to the slapping, groaning, smashing waves below. Connie had started back up the path to rejoin the group for the lighthouse tour, when the fog began to swirl sideways, and a battering of cold rain hit her face. She stumbled and slid down a slope into a hollow, came up against an enormous gun barrel, and with a cry of alarm, ran for shelter into the dark shadowy cavern behind it.

"It's drier back here, and you can share my cape," came a voice from the darkness. With foolish disregard for her safety, Connie felt her way along the rough concrete wall towards the voice.

"Hi," she ventured. "Are you a tourist too?"

He laughed. "Well, I'm not from these parts, if that's what you mean. I've just come off guard duty. What are you doing here? I thought the barracks was off-limits for ladies of the town."

Connie was confused and somewhat offended at being called 'a lady of the town', whatever that meant.

"Are you playing some sort of game with me?" she asked.

"Sure, we can play a game if you like. It helps to pass the time. How about Flip?"

"I don't think I know that one. I play Magic Duels, though. My online code name is Conjura. Do you have a name?"

"Corporal Magnus O'Reilly, Royal Canadian Artillery, at your service, Ma'am! I haven't really needed a code name, but how about you call me . . . Imaginus? Here's a coin, want to flip first?"

Conjura fiddled in her backpack for a flashlight, so she could read whether it came up heads or tails.

"Hey, this is an old coin. 1942. And it's a *Newfoundland* dime! This might be worth something."

"Yes, about ten cents, I'd say. Come on, toss!"

* * *

They were a strangely unmatched pair from behind: one tall and heftily built, his head of curly red hair poking in all directions from under his wooly hat, the other short and slim, with straight black hair drawn back over his head from his brow into a braided queue down his back.

("Yay, that's a tail for me! A queue is a pigtail!"

"Darn, you're right, but still two heads for me.")

Together they rolled up the street from Dublin Port, seeking to regain their land legs after a long voyage that had taken them from the South China Sea, around the Cape of Good Hope, and up the Atlantic coast to Ireland.

They had struck up a friendship after one of Seamus' bunk mates had accused Chan Ling Li of stealing tobacco from him. Seamus knew it couldn't be true, as he had seen Li choke and nearly throw up after trying a pipe of tobacco once. He grabbed Fritz round the neck and put a headlock on him before he could throw Li overboard. A search of the bunks found the missing plug tucked under the mattress, and all was calm again. Li was ship's cook, and afterwards he used to save tasty treats, like head cheese, for Seamus, and they soon became best mates.

Now they were making their way to a pub that Seamus knew well from his youthful Dublin days, to fulfil a promise he had made. Along the way they passed a barber's shop with its spinning candy stripe pole. There were half a dozen other sailors lined up inside, waiting to get their heads and chins trimmed and shaved after a long voyage. These days, not many favoured the braids and beards of former times. Seamus and Li walked right on by, one not caring, and the other already well coifed.

("I think the barber is a bit gratuitous, they don't even go in. You're just picking up another six easy points."

"Well, they're sailors, and they have probably been on the same boat."

"Hmm.")

As they approached the Liffey Arms, Seamus was extolling the virtues of his favourite tipple, qualities which had probably grown with the year or two since he had last tasted it. They pulled open the door and were met by a warm fug of smoke, sweat, salt, stale fat, and the saturating smell of ale. On the stained but polished wood counter, stretching the length of the saloon, stood a line of tall glasses. The first two were filled to the brim, a licorice black with a dense creamy head. The rest were being slowly topped up in turn, one pull of the tap at a time.

"Y'see, Li, if ye tried to fill the glass in one go it would foam all over the bar. It takes a good five minutes to pull a glass of Guinness."

"Seamus? Is that you lad? Found your way home then. There's a glass waiting for ye."

"Make that two, Liam. I promised my mate here that I would introduce him to the nectar of the gods when we reached Dublin Port."

Seamus had downed two glasses before Li had got much beyond the foamy head of his glass, but he persevered for his friend's sake and finally finished it. He was feeling a little green around the gills, as bad as the seasickness which had afflicted him on his first ocean voyage, and he needed Seamus' strong arm to guide him out the door.

By the time they were boarding the ship, Li was dizzy and beginning to retch. Seamus hurried him forward and thrust his head into the toilet just in time.

"Well, I hate to see a good pint wasted, but I guess your gods have a different nectar."

("So that's fourteen for me, eight for you."

"Wait a moment, I make it thirteen. *If* I let you count the heads in the barber's."

"You're forgetting what a ship's toilet is called!")

* * *

The fog cleared suddenly, and the watery sun shone intermittently from between the clouds. The tourist bus waited an extra ten minutes, but when there was no sign of the last passenger, it headed back to town. Later that day, the driver would file a report about the missing woman, and eventually, when no sign of her or her belongings was ever found, it was assumed she must have been swept off the rocks by a rogue wave as she stumbled about in the fog. Bodies are seldom recovered from these treacherous waters of the Atlantic on the eastern edge of the continent.

* * *

"That was fun," said Conjura. "Toss again. And how about beds or sails this time?" Imaginus flipped the coin, and it kept on and on spinning tales.

The End

Footnote:- A gun battery was installed at Cape Spear, Newfoundland, in 1941, to defend the entrance to St. John's harbour, and it was abandoned in 1945. A gun barrel and ruined barracks still remain.

CPSIA information can be obtained
at www.ICGtesting.com
Printed in the USA
LVHW050014080519
617050LV00001B/79